I0524410

THE HABITAT
RELOCATION PROJECT
By
Colin Setterfield

SURVIVAL OF A SPECIES

PART TWO

Paperback Book Edition

ISBN 978-1-988719-07-8

TABLE OF CONTENTS

PROLOGUE

Excerpt from the President Commander's Log.

18th June, 2367 CE

The Andromeda has been severely damaged by alien enemy fire. The Crustans are a war-like species from another dimension and are invading our universe for life support supplies and minerals. We are adrift and without power, protective shields are down, weapons will not prime. They will board us soon......

∞∞

One

A Sudden Ripple in Space-time.
July, 2323 CE

Deep Space is a total enigma. If you are not one to look at the dark void with the eyes of an astrophysicist it will translate the vacuum into a repetitive nothingness which goes on forever. Looking at the Cosmos this way provides no relief from the boredom spacers suffer, on long interstellar voyages. Sometimes circumstances will provide a diversion from the norm and throw in an emergency to relieve the monotony. Space is a dangerous place.

"Give me an update on the Solar Star, Gary."

"The onboard computer is not responding to any new instructions."

"Has the captain tried manual control?"

"Yes—no response from manual."

"How long until they get it sorted out?"

"They're working on it as fast as they can, Beckett. It will take diagnostics at least another hour before maintenance can even start a repair."

"Good—make sure they have isolated the object from the ore and send us an analysis of its constituents."

Lieutenant Commander Gary Pearson, Executive officer of the Andromeda, agreed. "I'll let you have the results as soon as I have them. Hopefully our diagnostics will be able to throw some further light on the molecular structure."

I turned back to the image on the holographic platform in front of me to resume my scrutiny of the FBO—Foreign Body Observation report. The Solar Star and its crew, engaged in normal Mineral extraction matters on one of the large asteroids, faced a dilemma. Without explanation, the onboard flight computer crashed after the unusual discovery of a mysterious object. It appeared in the aftermath of ore collection, to become an accessory with a myriad of splintered rocks, in the system's fragmentation nets. Nobody could verify the object's geological substance. Some thought it might have been manufactured—the preliminary scan of elemental composition suggested unfamiliar material. The object's strange shape attracted many stares and much bewilderment. No such object registered in the foreign body's data bases anywhere on Earth or with other galactic Mine organizations. The 1mx1mx2m sized artifact provided opportunity for many suggestions and generated much heated discussion amongst the scientists on board the Andromeda.

The malfunction of the Solar Star's computer, coincided with the on board storage of the mysterious object and may have seemed to be a coincidence, but to me it played a foreign note in the orchestral cosmic symphony. I would have to wait for the final analysis.

'Can I get you something to drink, Master Beckett?'

The android's digitized purr cut through the veneer of my thought and a tang of annoyance at the distraction raised my ire. I swiveled in the chair to confront the intrusion but caught my tongue in time, before the irritation mustered a reprimand—the android's sole ambition centered on my personal needs.

"Yes, thank you, Happydoo—it's about time I hydrated. Between you and Mrs. Carla, I feel like a pampered house cat."

Happydoo raised his bionic knuckles to his synthetic mouth and chuckled. *'I am happy to do it for you Master Beckett. I will bring you some hot cafteen'.*

The android has been a member of our family for a long time and undergone many upgrades to its quantum processor over the years. Whenever I look at Happydoo my thoughts return to the time I almost lost him for good. It happened shorly after my introduction to the crew of the Andromeda, under the command of my Uncle Sid Conroy at the time. My life, embarked on a directionless spiral because of the non-existent relationship between my father and I, took a turn for the better when my uncle took me under his wing.

My father's death took Uncle Sid and I back to Earth for the funeral, a difficult time for both of us. My dad, Padraig Conroy, a geneticist at the World Genetic Foundation, discovered a way to increase longevity by means of telomere integrity replenishment. His discovery became the target for selfish gain by one of his colleagues and the New World Earth Intelligence Agency. Both tried to steal the research left to me as a legacy. To cut a long story short, Happydoo became the eventual target of the NWEIA when they discovered his processor contained all the research for my dad's breakthrough. In a life and death confrontation with a NWEIA hit squad, Happydoo suffered almost complete annihilation.

Carla touched my shoulder with a soft, warm hand. "What's happening, honey?"

"I'm perusing the Foreign Body report, Sweetheart. The Hawking Probe has picked up a large gamma ray burst from a supernova nobody knew anything about."

"Would it be bad for our mining operation? I mean, aren't supernovas dangerous things?"

"A giant gamma ray burst could ultimately destroy the Earth's ozone layer completely, leaving the planet at the mercy of our sun's radiation."

"Do they know how long it would take the star to come within destructive range of Earth?"

"There is a whole group of scientists working on it as we speak. It's too soon to know if the trajectory will bring it close but It is hopefully still a long way off and we'll have time to develop a plan if we are in any danger."

Carla gave me a doubtful glance and moved over to the view port. "I hope for our sakes it doesn't make an appearance."

"Don't worry your pretty little head over it, Love. I'm sure we'll have plenty of warning. We do have another minor problem, though—an object of unknown composition showed up in the ore operation on one of the asteroids we're mining."

"Are you saying the object has no trace elements common to the asteroid?"

One of the many attributes I love about my wife is her ability to clue into difficult concepts with ease. We met under strange conditions when Uncle Sid and I visited Earth to pay our final respects to my dad. Carla, an undercover operative for the Intelligence Agency at the time, worked for the World Genetic Foundation. Her mission, to unearth the origin of threats against my dad before his death, brought us in contact with one another. She offered to help me in the search for my dad's lost research. I fell in love with her at first sight. She saved my life on more than one occasion and after I inherited Uncle Sid's business, the Galactic Mine Corporation, she consented to accompany me into space. We married a year later, aboard the Andromeda.

"The quality assurance guys will analyze the object but the prognosis so far suggests an unknown elemental composition. Because of this I am confident the object is manufactured and not geological."

"You think aliens might have visited the asteroid?"

"Once the age of the asteroid is known they will be able to determine if it once belonged to a planet or a supernova star fragment. The object might have been buried at the time of a planet's demise. Another possibility is it may have been left by an unknown alien presence."

Carla returned to drape her arms over my shoulders and observe the holo-report. "How long before we know?"

"Dr. Benson will brief me the moment the Solar Star returns. Hopefully he will have some answers by then." I didn't mention the fact of the shuttle's incapacitation because I deemed it only to be temporary.

The Andromeda is our world away from home. The spacecraft is huge. We can mine almost any type of material in the known universe and process the mineral content for storage. We mine gold, silver, tungsten, iron, iridium, platinum and a host of other metals. The Solar Star is one of ten shuttles used to ferry miners to and fro from the spacecraft. The occasional trip back to Mars or Earth is undertaken by the Excalibur, our long-distance shuttle, for furloughs and material delivery. At present, our compliment of miners is fifteen hundred people and we engage as many as twenty-one asteroids at a time—business is good.

The XO, Gary Pearson, appeared at my elbow. "Beckett, you're needed at the main console."

"What's up, Gary?"

"The Solar Star has vanished!"

∞∞

TWO

Lost In Space

"Impossible! How can a transporter the size of a small hotel just vanish?"

"I'm not sure. There's no indication it took off—it simply disappeared."

"What has happened to the crew?"

"As far as we can tell the relief shift had disembarked the vessel and are on the surface of the asteroid. The previous shift is all aboard, waiting for the techs to fix the onboard computer problem, hoping to be brought back to the Andromeda—there is no sign of them or the ship."

"Did anyone on the relief shift see anything?"

"Apparently no one can make head or tail of it. It's as though the Solar Star was never there. The relief crew boss says he remembers their arrival, disembarkation and the walk to temporary quarters. When he came out to start the shift the Solar Star was gone."

We arrived at the main console and a young ensign snapped to attention. Although the Galactic Mine operation is a commercial venture the Andromeda's crew adheres to limited, Navy-flight protocols while on the spacecraft. The miners and supervisors, organize along usual industrial factory lines.

It's been ten years since I took ownership of the business, an inheritance from my uncle, and the consequent command of the Andromeda. Before my uncle's demise I worked under him for a period of four months, prior to our brief return to Earth for my dad's funeral. My initial education, a basic course in genetics spawned of my father's will, in the hope I would follow in his footsteps, ended when I resisted the notion. Instead, I spent many years on the in-city beaches in a vain attempt to become a pro-surfer.

"What do you have for me ensign?"

"I have managed to obtain footage from a camera on the corner of the accommodation building, President Commander. It's the weirdest thing I've ever witnessed."

The ensign tapped a few keys on the console computer and the large platform at the end of the bridge sparked to life with a hologram. The picture showed the Solar Star at rest on its temporary propulsion platform, loaded up with the off-duty miners and the strange artifact. A delay followed, due to the sudden onboard computer problem after which, to my astonishment, the entire craft vanished into the non-atmospheric gloom.

"Replay that section," I barked at the ensign. "I can't believe what I just saw. It's impossible!"

The hologram viewed again with the same conclusion. Gary Pearson stood routed to the spot. Carla and the ensign stared in utter disbelief with their mouths agape in astonishment. The ensign played the holo several times before I managed to speak.

"It can't be a malfunctioning camera—look how the background appears as the vessel is disappearing."

Pearson offered a possible cause. "The strange object must have something to do with it."

"Carla found her tongue. "It's the only recently introduced anomaly. "

My mind computed the veracity of Carla's word and the ramifications of the incident hit me. Happydoo arrived to thrust a mug of cafteen into my hands.

"How many people aboard?"

Pearson signaled to the ensign and a holo-file appeared on the platform.

"One hundred and fifty-three, President Commander. The shift-boss is James Carter, a thirty-year veteran miner."

We all stood in somber silence and stared at the holo-file while I searched my knowledge of emergency protocol. An instruction, as per the abnormal nature of the incident, might lie within the provision for: "Vessels lost in Space,"—obscure, but the computer should be able to find it.

"Mickey—search the emergency protocol for the clause dealing with missing vessels."

Mickey, adapted from the acronym "MICS" or Master Interstellar Control System, is Andromeda's brains and central nervous system. The AI handles all the computerized actions aboard the vessel with the attitude of a personal super-secretary. A male persona characterizes the computer's digital personality and 'he' can handle any technicality of flight in space.

'At once President Commander. The clause is EP7600 and provision one states:

If a vessel is lost in space an immediate search for a heat signature must be undertaken. In the event there is no signature, the search-party should anticipate the lost vessel to be without power. The chief executive officer is to be informed and permission granted for a laser identification search.

"Thank you, Mickey. It makes perfect sense —please perform the two tasks mentioned in provision one and get back to me."

'Right away, President Commander'.

"Gary, pull off a list of all those on the Solar Star. If we don't find out what's happened to them I'll have to file a missing-person's report with the Interstellar Mine Association and the next of kin will need to be informed."

"Consider it done, Boss. Will you inform the rest of the Andromeda's crew about the incident?"

"I think it best we wait for Mickey to report back first. At least we'll know if this is a temporary situation or if it'll take a little longer to get to the bottom of things."

I knew the news would travel fast. The relief shift, still at the mine on Tiffany, would figure it out and try to communicate with family and friends aboard the Andromeda. I didn't want to keep anyone in the dark—the more information we could share, the better. They say undesirable incidents come in groups of three. With a possible neutron star on the way to our solar system and the disappearance of an entire shift of miners—what third catastrophe awaited me in the near future?

Carla came to me and placed her arms around my waist. "Don't worry, Hon. I'm sure there's a logical explanation for all of this."

We hugged each other for a few seconds until my need to be proactive got the better of me. I broke the embrace with a kiss on her forehead and moved to the view-port.

"I need to gather the mine managers together and explain the situation. It'll take Mickey a few more minutes to establish any possible signature, or laser ID search possibilities, so we might as well go ahead and get the departmental heads together for the brief.

"If there're no signs, what will you say to them?"

"I'll tell them the truth. The Solar Star has disappeared without explanation—with all the personnel and we'll be doing all, within our power, to find out what happened to them."

"Will you mention they took a foreign object aboard before the craft vanished?" asked Carla.

"I guess it would be wise to offer all the facts —we have no information of a link between the two incidents."

She folded her arms and we stared out of the view-port for a few moments before I made my decision.

"Mickey. When you've established the status of the Solar Star please make an announcement for all departmental heads—to meet me in the boardroom. I want all the mine managers and ranking flight officers to be present— immediately."

'At your service President Commander. I have, so far come up with nothing—no human or craft presence anywhere within workable parameters. Given the normal laws of physics a craft, moving away from us at the speed of light, could not have exceeded twenty light-minutes. I am searching up to thirty light-minutes in all directions—no human or rocket heat signatures so far.'

"Laser identification search?"

'No signal at all, President Commander.'

The XO glanced at me. "This is a very strange turn of events. We don't have any craft with such a speed capability. Excalibur can barely exceed .7 percent light-speed. No heat signatures or laser ID which means the craft is not anywhere within the search parameters."

"This is beyond the scope of our known physics, Gary. We'll need to be looking in other realms—I don't know how we'll be able to do that."

"What do you mean by 'realms'"

"I have a feeling the foreign object aboard the Solar Star is more than we anticipated it to be."

Gary Pearson raised his eyes to meet my stare. "Such as..."

"The notion, crossing my confused mind at this moment, is the word 'dimension'. I think our object could be some sort of time machine or dimension-jumper."

∞∞

Three

The Rehabilitation Project

The brief with departmental heads and mine managers lasted for two hours. The hushed atmosphere reflected the somber thoughts of those present and galvanized the scientific minded to speculate on the cause of the Solar Star's sudden disappearance. The head of astrogation pointed out the obvious.

"With all due respect, Sir—a vessel, the size of the Solar Star does not simply dissolve into the elements of space. It must be hidden behind something."

Gary showed the video and drew gasps of utter amazement. I dealt with the inevitable question of why the object needed to be brought in for closer inspection and not left on Tiffany. The truth about the omnipotence of hindsight is the bane of everyone's life, with regard to decisions based on limited background information. Every departmental head will acknowledge this. My reason for the object to be brought over to the Andromeda rested on the principles of economics and time—

our portable diagnostic equipment for field work is limited. The Andromeda's material analysis lab relied on samples taken from digs but the nature of the object negated a physical sample. The onsite diagnostics gave no indication of any danger.

Protocol demanded the incident be reported to the Galactic Mine Authority. Although this did not sit well with me I thought it prudent to advise them of the incident and to relate the facts, as far as we knew them, with a promise of a full report when more information became available.

At the close of the brief I headed to my office. The Solar Star could not have vanished—space-time still held many mysteries for us. Mickey might be able to shed some light on the dimension angle.

"Mickey. What do you have in your active memory regarding String theory?"

'The best contender for the theory of everything if I'm not mistaken, President Commander.'

"It's a guess but the more I think about it the more I favor it. I think our object has pulled off some sort of 'dimensional jump', taking the Solar Star with it—what do you think?"

'It does seem like a logical answer to the dilemma, President Commander. The String theory Hypothesis touts at least eleven available dimensions in the universe but so far no positive proof of this exists.'

"What would be required to exploit another dimension, other than the known ones?"

'I believe the achievement of a fifth dimension would require an almost infinite amount of power to be generated from a controllable source within the existing four dimensions of space and is not within our scope of practice or current knowledge, President Commander.'

"I feel so helpless, Mickey. I'm responsible for the Andromeda's people and it was my decision to bring the object aboard the Solar Star—I feel I've failed them."

'We are assuming the object had something to do with it, President Commander, but the truth is no one knows for sure. Never-the-less, it would be prudent to work on the reason's regarding your decision—the Galactic Mining Authority will demand it.'

"Keep 'pinging' the skies for an answer. Give me a report every half-hour."

'It will be done, President Commander'.

I decided to spend some time in the executive spa, to work on my body's acclimatization, one of the daily and mandatory requirements for all spacers. It would give me time to think about the "how", to word the future GMA report.

"I'll be in the gym if anyone is looking for me, Mickey."

'Very well, President Commander.'

I climbed into a pod and hooked myself to the spa computer and settled on the cot to await the commencement of the process. My mind soon became lost in thoughts of lost miners and the strange artifact-like object.

Two hours later a voice broke into my contemplations. I could see Gary's face through the clear graphene-glass cover of the pod. The cover sprang open at a touch of my finger on the inner console.

"What's up, Gary?"

"You are wanted at the main console. There's a message from Earth on the holo-platform."

"Who is it?"

"A Doctor Abrams from some project or other."

"Project—are you sure he wants to talk to me?"

"Asked for you by name and it's a she."

What's the time delay at the moment?"

"We are presently at the shortest possible distance between Earth and the asteroid belt so the delay will be approximately six minutes. The usual packaged conversation applies. I told Abrams you would be waiting for her next message."

"I'll be there in a few minutes—just need to unhook myself from the machine."

I hated packaged conversations but it's the way of all our space-Earth communications. A six minute delay meant a distance of about one-hundred million kilometers. All questions received answers on the return communication—there could be no actual flow of conversation. I anticipated an interview about galactic Mine operations and wondered what a relocation project might be after.

I needed an ablution to wash away the perspiration from the exertion of the workout and headed for the gym's demist cubicle. The wall-chrono showed 1904 hours, so Pearson's answer to the mysterious doctor would still take at least another three minutes before it reached Earth. Time still remained before a response to Gary's message came through to the Andromeda.

The mist in the ablution chamber cleaned away the sweat and the warm-air drier swirled an air current around my body. A new suit-coverall, selected from the auto-dress fabricator, took a few minutes.

Carla joined me at the console and at the same time Gary left to handle a staff issue in the maintenance department. I suggested the on-duty ensign take a refreshment break while Carla and I waited for Dr. Abram's response. Mickey stood by to receive the long-range signal from Earth.

'Message incoming, President Commander.'

The hologram materialized on the platform. An attractive, young woman smiled at us over the one-hundred million kilometer gap:

"Hello, Dr. Conroy. I bring you greetings from the New World Earth Relocation Project."

The name struck a bell in my memory. The NWERP, first called Spacewatch, gained sponsorship through NASA back in the old American super-power days. The group watched near Earth objects and large-bodied asteroids, considered a possible danger to the home planet. The Project published the foreign body report, which occupied me at the time the bad news of the vanished Solar Star, came to my attention.

"—my name is Lynette Abrams and I am currently head of the New World Earth Relocation Project. My contact with you is approved by The Administration's National Security Council and is a level one priority. I am sure you will have read our recent report about a giant gamma ray burst from a neutron star, which moved out of its original orbit in the Groombridge Area. This star—we have no name for it—remained hidden from telescopic view, behind Groombridge 183 until recently. Its supernova affected 183's position and gave our astronomical team its first look at the advent.

The supernova has caused the unknown star to collapse into a neutron body. By its nature it emits an immense amount of gamma rays and is headed straight for Sol's solar system. The Goombridge system is thirty light years away. This gives us a heads-up as to what can be expected down the road. The GRB can be weathered but it will completely destroy the Earth's ozone layer. The real bad news is the neutron star, now broken away from a binary system, is headed our way but is much slower than the GRB. When it arrives in our solar system all will change our habitable space. It means, President Commander, people on Earth and Mars need to find a new habitat.

Your Mine operation may not be greatly affected by the initial GRB but eventually you too will have to find a new region of space. Your ship, the Andromeda, is the largest of its kind and we would very much like you to consider a new project—to find our species a new home. If you are interested in this mission—to save the human race from extinction, please let me know in your return communication. Ask all the questions you need to —I and my colleagues will try to answer them as truthfully and honestly as we can. I look forward to it."

∞∞

Four

Decision Time

Carla and I stared at each other with incredulity as we tried to focus on what the NWERP message meant. The XO, returned to the Con and saw our startled expressions. He waited with raised eyebrows but when I continued to stare at Carla, his visage of enquiry dissolved into a grin.

"Are you two having a special moment or something?"

The sound of his voice broke the spell.

"We have just heard an incredible story. Dr. Abrams has asked us to be involved in a new project and it doesn't involve mining the asteroid belt."

"Who is she?"

"Head of the New World Earth Relocation Project. I read their NEO report minutes before the news of our lost miners became known. It seems this gamma ray burst is much more serious than we thought."

"What did she want from you?"

"The NWERP want us to be involved in finding a new habitat for the human race."

Gary Pearson frowned. "I thought that's what the terraforming of Mars was for."

"The GRB from the rogue neutron star is not the final problem. It appears the star has been ejected out of its binary system and is heading our way," I said.

"Shit! That does make a big difference but neutron stars don't travel fast. It must still be a long way off—would probably take a couple of hundred years to reach our solar system, so why the panic?"

"They feel the GRB will wipe out the ozone layer completely and that could happen within the next thirty years. While the human race already lives in dome-protected cities the planet will officially be dead. They feel we need to explore deep space and find an exoplanet we can inhabit and we need to start the process right away."

Carla interrupted the conversation. "The logistics of such an achievement with our present technology is nigh impossible. We are talking about traveling umpteen light years to find what we're looking for."

I understood her point. The Excalibur, our Earth shuttle, is the fastest of our spacecraft. It is the most advanced ship ever built, capable of .01 percent the speed of light, a fraction of the speed necessary to make interstellar travel a possibility.

We would need to find an exoplanet in orbit around a yellow dwarf star, similar to Sol and at about a distance of fifty light years from our present system.

"Dr. Abrams would have taken all this into account so there should be no need to point out the obvious—to have considered such an impossible task she must have something else up her sleeve."

"I'll be interested to hear about it," said Carla.

Gary Pearson agreed. "It sounds like an impossible task to me, unless they know something we don't."

My sense of intrigue flowered into full bloom to deal a blow to general skepticism of involvement with official government, or military endeavors. Maybe the thought of it flattered my ego. Any contemplation of such a life-change might be a result of the tediousness of the asteroid Mineral recovery process.

"I would like to arrange a quick return package for Abrams. Carla, can you make notes while we discuss the key questions that should be asked? We'll keep this between the three of us for the time being—until we know more."

The XO addressed the young ensign, who witnessed the entire message and consequent conversation. "You are now under strict orders not to divulge anything you have heard regarding this situation—not a word to anyone until further notice—is that understood Ensign?"

Pearson, Carla and I left the ensign at the console and retired to my office to organize the return message for Abrams. After ten minutes of intense discussion, on questions which might best inform us about the project, I glanced through Carla's notes. My body shook with excitement and anticipation, however, I must confess to a certain amount of trepidation. A decision in favor of the Project constituted the most drastic change imaginable. The final decision, which lay with me as the owner of the galactic Mine operation, would not be made with any ease. If my choice supported the Relocation Project I should hope for a strong agreement from the people I worked with. Everyone on board entertained relationships with Earth in one form or another—family, friends, property interests, retirement plans. All these relationships would, in an irrevocable sense, end or be altered. Many families onboard who returned to Earth on furlough included children. The converse of the family scenario played out with groups of singles and couples, who considered the Andromeda to be their permanent home. For them no real, cataclysmic change took place if the Earth ceased to exist.

"I think we're ready for Abrams now."

Our questions, specific and to the point, probed every aspect of the importance of our life-support, plus the problem of time verses velocity. We moved back to the main command console and handed the details to the ensign for transmission. He pattered nervous fingers over the command station computer's input keys while I sat in the captain's seat with my notes. The message took me about five minutes to execute and we relaxed for the space-communication delay to run its course. An answer to our questions could be expected within half-an-hour.

My mind flitted back to the lost miners. There seemed little we could do to resolve the issue of their disappearance

"Mickey; has there been any sign of the missing ship?"

'Sorry, President Commander—my efforts have not been rewarded in any way. I will continue to search.'

The thought of a "lost in space" report to the Galactic Mine Authority made me fell edgy. After a period of forty-eight hours this would, however, have to be done. The Agency would send a team of investigators to satisfy themselves as to the possible breach of protocols and procedures. They would sniff and snuffle through every communication to do with the tragedy—the lead investigator's verdict to be deemed complete when I, as commander, proved guilty of an irregularity.

"Dr. Abrams return package is now available, President Commander."

"Very well, Ensign—put it on the platform."

The hologram burst to life and Dr. Abram's face appeared. Her soft voice displayed a purpose and urgency, not sensed in her first communication.

"Greetings, Doctor Conroy. Thank you for responding so quickly to our request. I will answer your questions as honestly as I possibly can, based on the present knowledge at my disposal. Please feel free to query anything you do not understand or request more information on any particular aspect of the project—."

The four of us sat spellbound as Dr. Abrams spoke. At the end of the session all our queries appeared to have been answered. There remained little for us to request extra information for—I would do so if we decided to get on board with the project. She asked me to take my time in consideration of the project and to keep it confidential—not to advertise the fact of the request beyond my executive associates. A decision would be required by 1500 hours on the 21st of July, 2323—one week to frame our answer. Carla, Gary and I retired to my office to discuss the pros and cons of involvement.

Carla looked dubious. "This is a huge undertaking, Beckett. I doubt if any of the mining staff will want to be a part of it."

"I feel we are obliged to help our species survive. This involves every living person, be it on

Earth or out in space. There will be those who will prefer for someone else do the pioneering but at the end of the day, everyone is affected. For those who decline involvement there are fourteen galactic mining contractors in the region. Continuance of chosen, or preferable employment in mineral extraction would be ensured," I said.

"There will also be those who would jump at the opportunity to become pioneers," said Carla.

Gary Pearson agreed. "I've been XO of the Andromeda for over thirty-five years and all it's ever been is mining asteroids. I wouldn't hesitate to make a change if it came to that. It's a tremendous honor to be considered for such a challenge—to go where no human being has ever been before."

I looked at Carla. "What about you, Honey?"

Her beautiful, emerald-colored eyes twinkled in the overhead light. "I will go where you go, Sweetheart. I don't think we really have a choice in the matter. Your development of the A-Mortal gene has made it possible for humans to live a lot longer. It may take that neutron star several hundred years to reach our solar system but if we aren't alive when it arrives our children will certainly be."

Carla made a good point. I inherited my late father's research legacy in 2315. His final wish for my career, vested in my initial line of study as a molecular geneticist, would be to improve on his work. I, on the other hand, baulked at the idea but, in the end, came to terms with it—one could say destiny called out to me, loud and clear. Before induction as the Andromeda's CEO I spent a short period at the New World Earth Learning Institute to upgrade my qualifications in genetics in continuation of the legacy. The papers on telomere integrity extension published several years later earned me my doctorate degree. Because of the breakthrough, initiated by my father and concluded by me, the human race life expectancy is now close to 200 years.

A new challenge flourished in the light of Carla and Gary's positive attitude.

"I knew Dr. Abrams had something up her sleeve, with regards to the time and distance problem we face. The NWE military's latest innovation will certainly help bridge the gap."

The XO leaned back in his chair and raised an eyebrow. "They've kept it a secret for ten years, no doubt waiting for the right time to announce their latest triumph."

"It couldn't have come at a better time. What did Dr. Abrams call it—Nuclear Pulse Propulsion?"

"It sounds extremely dangerous. I'm not sure I want to be sitting on top of several nuclear bombs," said Carla.

I smiled at her discomfort. "It may be dangerous but their trials have shown it can be done.

Seventy-five percent the speed of light is a huge breakthrough for interstellar travel."

"We may still have to resort to a form of intermittent hibernation for the distance though," the XO contested.

I glanced at Carla and winked. "I think we may solve that problem quite easily."

Pearson frowned, about to ask what my answer meant, but thought better of it. Little did he know; Carla and I shared a dark secret from the days we spent on Earth before our involvement in leadership of the galactic mineral extraction operation.

∞∞

Five

A Sealed Deal

The content of our discussions with the executive leadership raged back and forth for five days. The executive consisted of all ranked officers of the flight crew, plus the three section managers of the mineral extraction venture.

The debate, of continued mineral extraction verses the relocation project, became quite heated at times but everyone knew it would be the owner of the corporation who made the final decision. As President Commander and owner of the corporation the final responsibility and decision rested on my shoulders. Tempted at some years back, to float shares in the company and gain more funds for the extension of the operation to the Kuiper Belt, I fortuitously declined the notion. Although suitable for most types of enterprises a board of directors might place a limit on the devolution of our assets—I know he would never have approved such a move during his tenure as owner. With a director's board our decision-making process could easily have become bogged down over the years, and in consideration of recent developments, we might not have gained enough votes for the relocation project. Another corporation, similar to ours, would gain the opportunity of involvement.

Carla, Gary Pearson and I, along with about twenty percent of the Andromeda flight executives, carried the torch for change. The Mine managers came out against involvement in the project, for reasons of job-loss and fear of the unknown. Everyone believed in the necessity of the relocation project but not inclusive of the Andromeda's involvement.

In the end I gained sufficient support from the flight crew to pursue the relocation venture. Dr. Abrams ensured me a lottery could be held for pro-project miners to be included in the final number of people who would be chosen for the venture. She also ensured me I would remain as president commander and Gary Pearson would retain his position as XO, but with one provision— we agree to include a member of the NWERP project team as an advisor and chief officer of the project's logistics. Carla and I experienced a sense of relief when the decision became final—we would be travel into deep space, further than anyone before us.

Elation at the step taken countered the sadness of departure from our norm. To part ways with the galactic mineral extraction venture meant a complete change of direction for everyone. The monumental wealth of credits, built over the years, through the mining of asteroids, found a new ownership in distribution to all current members of the flight crew and the denizens of Andromeda City. Those who chose to leave us did not go empty handed but received huge bonuses. Our ties with mother Earth, however, and the system of business exchange would soon be forever altered. The Andromeda would rely on its own resources—the people onboard and the functions they performed, plus yield from the harvest of resources in space. The past extraction of minerals in space taught us much about the harvest of life-support energies for the future.

The night after the final meeting, Carla and I drained of emotion, prepared for bed. My wife's concerns about leadership of the new venture, required greater clarification.

"The advisor is an android?"

"Android's have come a long way, Sweetheart. I mean look at Happydoo, especially since his last upgrade—how sophisticated he has become; almost human."

"I realize that but the thought of taking advice from a machine is a bit disconcerting for me," she said.

I tried to placate her reservations. "The android in question is the project's representative on The NWE Administration forum. For a machine to hold such a high position is a remarkable achievement—it shows how clever those programmers are. The project needs The Administration's financial input to fund the propulsion system."

The Administration is the brains of the New World Earth strategy and runs all global affairs. It also manages world economics and is a developer of policies to uphold the peace through a global police and military initiative. It is also an intelligence gathering organization. The Administration also kept tabs on all issues and systems through a super computer called "Central."

Carla pouted. "This android is the only aspect of the project I have a problem with but Abrams did make it clear you are in charge. I guess I will have to trust your instincts—besides, I'm still head of security which means I can keep an eye open for any potential problems."

"That's my girl. You're the very best Carla. As an ex member of the New World Earth Intelligence Agency I'm sure nothing ever gets by you."

She smiled at my inference to the NWEIA. Her knowledge of stealth projects, covert operations and secure systems made her a natural recipient of the security detail aboard the Andromeda. I knew she would be more than adequate to handle the challenges of the new venture.

"The Andromeda will need a complete refurbish to make way for the new propulsion system. It will take several months to make the alterations and inclusions needed for interstellar travel."

"When you addressed Gary's question about hibernation during interstellar flight you winked at me—I assume you alluded to your dad's final discovery when you said the problem might be easily resolved?"

"Yes. To transfer the consciousness of hibernating personnel to a consciousness retention vial would ensure the individual's continued flow of thought—CRV's would be hooked into a computer stimulation of the neuron and synapse functions pertaining to memory."

"What happens with memory over the hibernation period?"

"The computer assimilation program feeds each brain with a memory in accordance with the individual's station in life—according to my dad's research the CRV computer will provide all sorts of virtual human experiences, and learning experiences for each mind to be occupied with. Our minds will experience normal stasis over the full hibernation period." I said.

"The thought of it scares the life out of me. How does the consciousness handle the fact of there being no physical body to operate through for such long periods of time?"

"It's an unknown. If you can remember, my dad's trial lasted over a period of about a week—but a successful transfer from the body to a CRV and back again was accomplished."

Fatigue from the week's tensions set in and we drifted off into a restless sleep.

*

The next morning I prepared a package for Dr. Abrams, in acceptance of the challenge. Our entire flight crew, a compliment of fifty-four people decided to stay with the Andromeda while one-hundred and eighty five Mine families, a compliment of five-hundred and forty two people, chose to join us. One hundred families gained acceptance through the lottery system devised by the NWERP.

The Galactic Mine Corporation would cease to exist once everyone received their severance credits and alternative employment found for all those who chose to go their own way. All mineral extraction operations needed to be terminated—there remained a huge amount of loose-ends. The company's law firm, Callas and Fincham, in Quantum City, would process all the required legal work.

Carla and I needed to travel back to the home planet for finalization of the new contract and to make provision for the Andromeda's retrofit at the space station, in orbit around Mars. There remained one important factor: the lost miners.

"Mickey, any trace of the Solar Star?"

'Negative, President Commander. However, there is an unusual anomaly being picked up by the heat signature sweep. It is a trace of friction-plasma, a residue of particle rupturing caused by an extremely high source of energy emanating from one specific spot directly above Tiffany.'

"Do you suspect it's related to the disappearance of the shuttle?"

'I cannot say, President Commander but I would be inclined to think so—there is nothing in space I know of that would leave such a residue.'

"Is there anything you might hypothesize to humor me?"

'Hypothetically, my thoughts go to an unknown source of energy existing along a fault-line in space—a sort of entrance to another dimension, however, this is purely speculative, President Commander.'

"Keep working on it. We cannot just give up."

'I will keep you posted, President Commander.'

∞∞

Six

February, 2324 CE

"Are we all systems go, XO?"

"All systems go and main reactor has reached peak load, President Commander."

"Begin main burn."

"Main burn started—T minus 09 seconds and counting."

The Andromeda quivered and shook like an old-fashioned combustion engine on loose mountings. I reminded myself of the normality of the phenomenon.

So much water under the bridge—the past six months saw unprecedented changes to the lives of the Andromeda flight crew. The intense instruction for the relocation venture left all participants with little time to think of the dangers ahead. Carla and I, our minds stretched to the limit, experienced great relief after graduation from the special knowledge induction courses foisted upon us as the leaders of the mission. The overall preparation for interstellar spaceflight turned out to be a huge undertaking for the administrators of the project.

Everyone needed to be prepared, both from a physical and psychological point of view, for three major aspects of our journey: Adaption to a different force of gravity for the duration of the trip, headed the list. In second place came orientation with the host of new systems and innovations to do with nuclear propulsion. The final aspect dealt with the pioneer mindset. To leave the comforts of mother Earth behind and live a great portion of one's years in space flight is a daunting contemplation. The consolation is the life-extension breakthrough, which adds an expectancy of years equal to the time we would spend on the journey. The prospect of life on another Earth-like planet, many light-years from our solar system, also played its part in our departure from the present zone of comfort. For those of us who already lived most of our lives in space, thought of concerns for the journey held less of a distraction—never-the-less, we needed to compute the enormity of our decision.

"T- minus three seconds. Prepare for major thrust—reactor is at full power.... -minus two, -minus one—we have break-away."

The vibration fell away as the huge magnetic restraints released and the Andromeda rocketed away into the darkness of space. The retro-fit station, in its orbit around the Red Planet, diminished in size on the viewing screen above my head and with it the last sight we would ever have of the planet Mars.

The take-off experience would have crushed all of us to a pulp but for the new acceleration compensation system. After fifteen minutes we attained seventy-five percent of light speed and the canopies, on our protective acceleration-pods, opened to liberate some of the flight crew for important duties. All other occupants remained in their pods and would remain there until Mickey set them free for medical checkup. Many of the families came from Earth-bound jobs, the relocation project the first time ever in a spacecraft. Others boasted long term space experience. No one aboard ever faced such an aggressive acceleration before, which made a post-pod release medical exam, mandatory for all.

The ship's company included two-hundred and fifty families of three to five people, one hundred and twenty couples, three hundred and twenty-five singles plus the flight crew—twelve hundred and sixty-five people in all.

"How's our new propulsion equipment holding up, Mickey?"

'There are no signs of any problems, President Commander. Seventy-five percent of light speed is attained and all systems are functioning as they should be. The remaining compliment of spacers will be released from their pods on a pro-

gressive basis—this will assist in the logistics of the medical examinations.'

Gary Pearson, whose release corresponded with mine, settled down in his seat at the Con. "I'm struggling a little with this new gravitational force."

"It will take some getting used to, so don't overdo things to start with. 1.3 times our normal Earth gravity is no big deal when you've spent as much time as we have in space."

"Yeah—you're right, Beckett. It's a bigger deal when one's been used to the fifty percent G we've mined asteroids under all the years, though."

Initiation of the life-aboard continuum program became a reality. A turn-key process awaited everyone after completion of medical examinations. The program saw to day-by-day involvement in a fiscal, production and recreational environment activities, as practiced back on planet Earth. For many it would be a return to the grind of their expertise and for others it would be a new vocation altogether. Apart from the flight crew, doctors, nurses, accountants, shop owners and producers of food made the bulk of the ship's compliment. The Andromeda posed the realities of a small city —with people, to churn out the essentials and non-essentials of day-to-day existence. Each person worked toward the best lifestyle affordable, compliments of their credits and work status. The spacecraft sported four movie theatres, twelve restaurants, twenty bars plus a host of other recreational facilities. The refurbished City area provided as much home comfort and ambiance possible under the circumstances—it remained for the individual to make it home.

A consul com-light blinked at me; a communication from the ship's infirmary. "President Commander, please report for your medical. Doctor Simons will see you immediately."

I nodded at Gary. "You have the Con. I'll be back shortly."

*

Thirty-six hours later the entire ship's company reported to their various stations of duty and apart from sixteen people, all passed the medical exam. The twelve medical doctors aboard did a great job with the workload, despite the new gravity constraints. Those who failed the exam required a longer rest period with extra time in the health-systems spa, under the care of the four resident fitness coaches.

Carla and I sat together at the main console in front of the holographic platform and viewed our immediate external surroundings. "How far have we come now, Hon?" She asked.

"You see the figure on the left? It gives the distance in astronomical units—we are a distance of 315 AU from Mars."

"I still can't grasp the fact we will never see our home planet again. It's like a nightmare gone wrong."

"Get used to it, Babe. This is a one-way journey like none other."

She smiled. "I know, Love—I will eventually but my mind is still largely Earth-bound."

"For every hour we travel, eight-hundred and ten million kilometers is added to the distance. You'll feel better in a few weeks because the distances will become too great to compute in your mind. It's best to start practicing looking ahead—to our new home."

"The constellation of Pegasus is fifty light years away. It's still too great for me to compute anything. What does that mean at our present rate of travel?"

"According to Einstein's special theory of relativity, time for us slows down significantly the closer we approach the speed of light. At .75C only forty-five years will have passed on the Andromeda in comparison to more than seventy years on Earth. We can be thankful for the hibernation periods or we would all go crazy. Mickey has it all worked out."

Carla ran a hand through her long blonde hair. "I understood half the ship's compliment is always on a sleep period, while the other half enjoys a normal life routine—is that the way it works?"

"You're so clever, Babe."

She grinned. "I'm not just another pretty face. I know these details were discussed at the beginning of our training but so much has been crammed into my mind since then."

"You might remember Dr. Abrams telling us about the two groups and how many years each would spend in hibernation—you and I, being in group A will spend seven years less than the group B, which is Gary's," I said.

"So...we'll be in hibernation for only fourteen years to Gary's twenty-one?"

"It will certainly help pass the time. Our group will have seven more years of wakefulness."

Gary Pearson laughed. "But just think about it—my group will have an extra seven years of sleep."

*

Forty-eight Hours Later

An alarm buzzer blared on the console, a stark intrusion to the cacophony of the bridge's normal, low-audible sounds. Gary Pearson looked at the forward visual display.

"There's something headed our way, President Commander. I'm not sure what it *is*—Mickey? Can you confirm what the foreign object's detection beam is picking up?"

'It appears to be made up of many small objects, Lieutenant Commander. I believe it is a swarm of asteroids and star debris, travelling together; the largest being two kilometers wide and the smallest, three meters across.'

"Can we alter our trajectory and bypass the swarm?"

'I'm afraid we cannot avoid them altogether, President Commander. The swarm is extremely large at the back-end—four AU across. I am taking evasive action in fifteen minutes. The Foreign Body Analysis detector is finding the least populated area—where most of the smaller objects are located. A critical path is being plotted as we speak.

The XO scowled. "How come the FBA is only picking this up now?"

'The FBA picked up the grouping shortly after launch but because of there being only a few large bodies up front obscuring the rest, the extent did not become evident until a few minutes ago, Lieutenant Commander.'

"Will our protective force-field be able to withstand the impact from the smaller rocks?"

'Time will tell, President Commander. I am issuing a general alert for everyone to enter the protective emergency pods immediately. I advise you to do the same.'

∞∞

Seven

Overcoming the Odds

The specific design of an emergency pod, in the event of severe damage to the spaceship, provides its occupants with ultimate protection. Groups of one hundred spacers are accommodated in each pod and, in the case of a main-craft breakup, operates under its own main computer authority. Everyone knew their designated pod and would go to the dedicated, emergency escape area in the center of the ship, if required.

I grabbed Carla by the elbow. "We're in Mickey's capable hands now—let's get to our designated pod."

The bridge emptied of all its occupants and we made our way to the verticap which services the designated emergency area. Streams of people poured in from all directions, on the move toward for the central area of the Andromeda. Within twelve minutes the entire ship's compliment of spacers snuggled together in their specific pods to await the sudden change in velocity and trajectory. The commander's pod accommodated twenty of the senior flight crew members plus Carla and I—

we enjoyed more space and luxury plus a dedicated holographic platform.

"Now I see what Mickey was talking about. Look at the size of those asteroids and how close they are to each other."

"What'll happen if the distances between the smaller ones are also small? We can't hope to maintain a critical path without impacts," asked Carla.

"Don't worry sweetheart. The shields will at least take the brunt of any impacts. I doubt whether they will be breached by the smaller rocks. The critical path includes the analysis of size, velocity and structure of dangerous rocks in relation to the strength of the shields protecting us. Any rock posing a real problem will be obliterated by the main forward laser."

She snuggled against me, rested her head on my shoulder and closed her eyes, to avoid the sight of the holographic images. "How long will it take to get through the swarm?"

"It's an extremely large swarm—about 5 Au deep. I don't think we've ever recorded one so large in space. If you look at the hologram you will see several numbers on the bottom-left—it shows a figure, 5.76 AU. That's how far we have to travel before break through. At our present speed it will take about fifty-five minutes to an hour."

Carla didn't bother to look at the platform. "It will be the longest hour of my life."

90 seconds later the acceleration comp system kicked in and an invisible hand squeezed on our chests. The Andromeda lurched to one side on the application of the critical path selection and we careened off at a different trajectory. Red colored figures tumbled on the platform as we closed in on the wall of asteroids. A second or two later the asteroids commenced a continual bombardment of the spaceships protective shields.

No sound emanated from the outside of the craft as hundreds of smaller rocks between three and ten meters hammered into the shield's triple layer force-field. The shudder of equipment and goods from the cargo deck could be heard with each strike. Carla's eyes opened wide as the ship weaved from side to side for a period of time. We endured strike after strike, until it came to an abrupt end.

"I believe we've survived the onslaught," I said.

A row of red alarm lights blinked from the main console; an indication of systems affected or knocked out.

"Mickey—damage report, please!" My voice sounded a bit strangulated.

'We have lost visual on the right-hand side of the vessel, President Commander. My hull sensors are showing a definite breach in one area, Section C42, which I have already isolated. There is a fire in the main propulsion reactor room—the

coolant to one of the reactors has been shut down and we are in danger of reaching critical temperature.'

"Have you alerted the fission techs?"

'They have been released from their pods and are on route to the propulsion room, President Commander. I have issued a directive for the mainstream to remain in their pods for the time being.'

"I am making my way to the bridge, Mickey. Please keep me updated."

Carla and I ran for the verticap. Gary Pearson arrived as we entered the capsule.

"That was fucking scary, wasn't it?" He said.

"A little bit too close for comfort—can you grab a detail and check out section C42? Mickey says the hull has been breached but is now isolated."

"For shit's sake, that's where we keep all medical and pharmaceutical inventory," said Gary.

"Well, we may have nothing left. You know what happens when any part of a pressurized hull is breached—."

"It could be worse, Beckett—next door to the breached store areas are our valuable supplies of hafnium reactor rods, for instance. If we lost those we would really be in shit street."

"I'm more concerned about the fire in the propulsion room. If we don't get immediate control there we won't be needing the rods."

The verticap ascended to the bridge area and we disembarked to see rows of red, lights on the blink. The senior con ensign arrived, his face a picture of concern.

"Switch on the holo of the propulsion room reactor coolant, Ensign. Let's have a look at what we are dealing with."

The hologram did not herald any good news. Heavy smoke interspersed with flame, blocked our view of the affected area. Several of the fission techs, tried to launch a stationary fire-bot in a flurry of confused action—each screamed instructions at the other. The fire-bots auto-mobilized on the detection of flames or excessive heat and this particular specimen, due to its malfunction, blocked off the narrow entrance to the coolant control area.

Mickey broke our intense concentration. 'The main overhead fire-suppressant system valve is damaged, President Commander. There is a connection from the drinking-water system which I am commissioning to bye-pass the damaged area to feed the emulsion coagulator. This is the only backup liquid supply for the system. We will lose much of the drinking water but it's our only chance of getting the fire out.'

"How long will it take for the water to be turned into fire depressant?"

'Three minutes, president Commander—but then we should have a steady supply for at least three hours.'

"Do it, Mickey—we can always make more water."

I returned my attention to the holo on the receiver platform. The techs could not budge the errant fire-bot so they resorted to hand-held suppressors, which amounted to a piss on a forest fire. The flames appeared to have blossomed in a connection box, loosened by the violent shudders of the Andromeda when it passed through the asteroid swarm. The water supply conduit above the box, melted due to the intense heat. This in turn shut off the coagulant tanks and supply to the fire-suppressant emulsion nozzles.

The fire did not, however, constitute the greatest danger. The violence of the asteroid strikes must have disturbed the alignment of the first reactor's coolant flow valves and caused them to shut off the supply of coolant. There are three giant reactors which deliver power to the Andromeda's central energy distribution rockets and drive the craft in take-of, increased velocity or changes of trajectory. A meltdown in any one of the three would seriously hamper the operation of the spacecraft.

'The backup water supply to the coagulators is now working, President Commander. We will have fire suppressant operation within twen-

ty seconds. The temperature in Reactor A is reaching critical level.'

"That's good news, Mickey—if we can quickly get the fire under control the techs will be able to get to the coolant, flow valve signal attenuators."

I waited for the suppressant system to energize again and after an eternity, thin streams of coagulant spouted from the nozzles bit to my consternation the blanket of emulsion did not retard the fire. I glanced at the reactor temperature—it continued to climb and I realized if the techs could not reach the valve attenuators within the next ninety seconds we would have a major catastrophe on our hands.

"What the fuck's happening, Mickey? The fire-suppression emulsion is not working."

'I am working to find the problem, President Commander. It seems that the drinking water refinement might have changed the emulsion's density and rendered it ineffective. There is only one thing we can do to put the fire out—remove the breathable air from the propulsion section and flood it with inert gas.'

I froze. "But what will happen to the techs? There isn't time to evacuate the section."

'We can only hope to get to them as quickly as possible. I have alerted the emergency rescue squad—they have already suited up and are on the move toward the propulsion room.'

We risked the potential loss of the four techs who did not have life support suits, if Mickey flooded the section with inert gas. There appeared to be no other alternative. A reactor meltdown would place the entire project in jeopardy.

Another glance at the temperature in the reactor galvanized my decision. "Activate removal of breathable air."

'Our chief android technical supervisor is standing by to approach the coolant valve attenuation section the moment the fire is out, President Commander.'

"Thank you Mickey. Please keep an eye on the emergency rescue and make sure there are health professionals available to assist when the techs are in a safe place."

I watched the holo. The fission techs fell to the ground, almost in unison as the inert gas rushed into the section. The fire died and I could see the emergency team, suited and on the move to extract the techs. Another figure raced through the smoke—Chief Spanner, the android in charge of robotic technical maintenance.

∞∞

Eight

Beating the Odds

Chief Spanner released the attenuation cover above the valve control system. Impervious to the lack of breathable air the android scanned the valve signal attenuators, through micro-camera eyes linked to the schematics in his processor. The temperature reached the point where the inside of the reactor started to melt.

A few seconds later he discovered the problem and reset the valve diaphragms to re-align the system for operation again. The valves opened in unison and coolant gushed through the warped tubes. I continued to watch as the temperature climbed a few more degrees before the red line peaked and levelled off. The sense of imminent disaster dissipated but left me weak at the knees. The project would have come to an abrupt end due to a full rupture of the reactor, tantamount to a limited nuclear explosion. The damage needed to be assessed and a plan for the repairs established.

Spanner replaced the attenuator cover and checked the rest of the coolant system. Satisfied no further damage to the process would occur he walked to the main panel where manual operations could be performed on the propulsion equipment. The temperature in the reactor fell to an acceptable level but the tubes, strained beyond their limits of normal operation, required replacement. The entire propulsion process needed to be terminated.

"What are our present power requirements, Mickey? Can we make the trajectory change needed to get back on our original course?"

'All three reactors need to be operating in order for the Andromeda to return to its original path, President Commander. The repair of Reactor A will take sixteen hours, inclusive of the two hours wait for it to cool.'

"What are the logistical implications of our remaining on the present trajectory for the duration of the repair—in distance and time?"

'We will be adding another two light years to our journey, President Commander.'

Carla spoke for the first time since the fire. "We can choose to remain in hibernation for the extra time. I guess it can't be helped."

I agreed with her. The situation might have been far worse—a ruptured reactor and a lethal contamination of the ship, not to mention the unknown devastation a nuclear explosion, even though vented out to space, would have caused.

"Is there any radiation contamination beyond the reactor?"

'None that my sensors can detect, President Commander. When everything has cooled down

sufficiently I will have the area re-pressurized for repairs to take place.'

With the imminence of a disaster now averted I stretched my legs. "Gary you have the Con. I'm going to check on the fission techs—Carla?"

"I'll go with you—just hope it's good news."

We grabbed the verticap and dropped three decks to the propulsion room escalator. An emergency First Aid post, outside the main entrance of the isolated area, served as the resuscitation clinic for the embattled techs. On arrival an air of tension saturated the atmosphere.

Two of the techs appeared to be out of danger with Chief Spanner and one of the security personnel in close attendance. The other two, a man and a woman, lay locked in the tentacles of the life-support revival module.

The doctor in attendance glanced at Carla and I as we approached. "This is going to be touch and go, President Commander. She's a tough one—the last to be brought in for resuscitation."

I could see the girl's dark hair and judged her to be about thirty years old. "What is her name."

"Laura Samuels."

Carla lent forward, and ran her hand through the dark curls. I could see the concern etched on her face.

"She appears to have suffered some burns."

The doctor agreed. "I believe she will be alright, providing the support module can restart the heart and stabilize the vital systems within the next minute. Her body is in deep shock."

While Carla stayed with Tech. Samuels I moved to the other victim. The attendant doctor shook his head. "We've lost this one, President Commander."

A wave of sorrow engulfed me as I knelt beside the man, still hooked up to the life support module. The realization of personal complicity in his demise weighed upon me and I fought to hold back my tears. "His name?"

"Brent Samuels, President Commander."

"Are they related?"

"Husband and wife," he answered.

For a second I wondered if it would be better for her to join her husband, and then guilt overtook me. Life is sacred to us all—we do not have the right to contemplate the fate or welfare of other beings. It will be tragic for her to lose her husband but her own life, in the end, is as precious to her as it is to us.

I moved over to the survivors. The first, an older man in his fifties, lay on his back, his eyes focused on the ceiling. 'Tech. Ron Blaise', printed on a tag, caught my eye and I grabbed his hand. "How do you feel, Ron?"

His bloodshot eyes held mine for a brief second in recognition. "I am feeling much better now, thankyou President Commander."

"I assume you realize what happened to you in the final moments of the fire?"

"I understand, President Commander—you had to make a difficult call."

"I'm afraid there was no other way out of the situation. For the good of everyone aboard it remained the only choice."

The tech looked over at the deceased man, now released from the support module. "It may not have been the best decision for him but I know it was the correct one under the circumstances."

I shook his hand again and moved on to the last survivor, a young man of about twenty-five years. You okay, Tech?"

"I'm good, President Commander."

I smiled and moved back to where Carla waited still with Laura Samuels hand in her own. I must have looked crestfallen because she reached out and pulled me toward her.

"I know how bad you feel, Beckett. Nobody blames you for the action you took. There are going to be casualties, no matter what we do."

"I know, hon—just can't help feeling bad about it though."

The ship's intercom burst into life and Gary's voice echoed within the confines of the hallway. "President Commander Conroy—to the con please."

I turned to Carla. "Stay here with her. I'll be back as soon as I can."

It took me several minutes to get to the verticap and a few more to arrive on the bridge at the main console.

"What's so urgent, Gary?"

The XO glanced gestured with his eyes toward the holo-platform.   The depicted scene caused me to do a double-take.

∞∞

Nine

An Unexpected Turn of Events

"What am I looking at here?"

Gary Pearson ran a sinewy hand through his greying mousy-colored hair. "It looks like a craft of some sort."

I glanced at the telemetry at the bottom of the holo. "It's still too far away for the system to identify the shape. Mickey—is there a signature?"

There is a heat signature, President Commander. The object definitely possesses a power system but not one known to our technology.'

"You're saying it's an alien craft with a power source too advanced for us to identify?"

That is what I'm saying, President Commander. The craft, if that is what it is, appears to be reducing velocity—almost as if it were allowing us to catch up.'

The XO stared at the platform. "How amazingly convenient—it seems to be right smack in front of us—how long until we're able to identify the shape, Mickey?"

The craft is at maximum range for our equipment, Lieutenant Commander. It is presently five hundred million kilometers distant, a little more than 27 light-minutes. We need to be at twenty light-minutes for a positive identification. I am working on an algorithm to predict a better observation time—if the craft's reduced velocity remains constant.

My mind flitted back to the fission techs. "I'm going back to the emergency revival station to join Carla. We've had one fatality and there might still be another—I need to be there."

"I have the con. We'll let you know what transpires when a positive ID on the alien craft is made," said Gary,"

*

When I arrived back at the emergency station, Carla's arm cradled Laura Samuels's shoulders. The girl looked pale but alive. The others gathered around the deceased tech, Brent Samuels and each touched his shoulder in a last gesture of farewell. I did the same. A crew of four men arrived to remove the body to the State room, where it would be prepared for a space burial. I moved over to Carla and Laura. "How are you feeling Mrs. Samuels?"

She turned her teary eyes on me and for a moment stared without recognition. "I'm alive, but Brent—"

Her words faded away as grief gave way to sorrow and tears flowed in a steady stream, over her pale cheeks. Carla tightened her hold and pulled the bereft woman to her bosom. There would be no words of comfort to pacify her vanquished soul. The two medics sensed the awkwardness of the moment and asked Carla for permission to take Laura to the clinic.

After they left, Carla turned to me with tears in her own eyes. "She wanted to know what 'fucking idiot' gave the order to depressurize and remove all the breathable air."

Carla's message stung like fiery hornets. "What did you say?"

"I said I would find out and let her know."

"Is she saying it wasn't necessary?"

"She intimated they might have been able to get a hold on the fire and put it out."

"She, unfortunately, doesn't know how close we were to disaster. I could not have waited another second."

"Don't fret yourself, honey. The poor girl has just lost her husband—she'll learn the truth in good time."

Carla's words did little to placate my concerns. Others might not agree with my actions. I decided to push the problem to the back of my mind.

"What did the bridge want you for?" she asked.

I told her about the strange craft. "I never imagined we would encounter anything like this but it's out there—possibly little green men."

Her face glowed with sudden excitement. "I can't wait to find out more about it. What will we do if we overtake it?"

"Investigate, of course. It might mean slacking off to whatever speed it's travelling—however, let's not forget we have a huge repair on the reactor ahead of us. Our priority is to get the Andromeda back to its full power potential."

"It will be a huge problem if the techs can't fix the propulsion system—without it we'll not be able to return to our present speed, if you slow the Andromeda."

Mankind, in its short tenure of space-flight, lacked an alien contact of any kind; this would be the first opportunity and I did not want to forgo it no matter what the reason. There remained little doubt in my mind we would be capable of the damaged reactor's repair.

"We'll cross the bridge when we come to it, Sweetheart. I'm waiting for Mickey to make an ID and possible contact figures—then we'll know where we stand."

The ship's intercom blared to life. "President Commander—please return to the bridge at your earliest convenience."

Carla and I clambered onto the escalator and headed for the verticap. On the bridge Gary awaited our arrival with an air of expectancy. "Mickey has some news for us." We fixed our eyes on the holo-platform. Mickey's digitalized purr filled the air around us.

'I have the algorithm in place, President Commander. We will meet with the alien craft in one hour and four minutes, providing its velocity reduction does not change. We are coming into range for positive ID.'

We stared at the holo, our eyes fixed on the blob of light, ahead of the Andromeda. The form-lessness of the craft materialized into a more solid structure and we saw its real shape for the first time.

"Holy crap," Gary shouted.

I gazed at the holo in fascination. "Shit—It can't be—tell me I'm dreaming."

∞∞

Ten

The Surprise of a Lifetime

"Mickey—please tell me it is what I think it is."

'If your thoughts are focused on the Solar Star, you would be correct, President Commander.'

My mind lapsed into a whirlpool of conjecture. The Solar Star, lost in space for seven months and presumed unrecoverable, floated in space ahead of us. How could this be?

"This is extraordinary. Our eyes must be deceiving us—have you confirmed it's the Solar Star and not an illusion, Mickey?"

'Everything checks out, President Commander. I have detected the anomaly again—the same trace of friction-plasma, the residue of particle rupturing caused by the recent presence of a very high energy—in the craft's wake.'

Once again, my mind reverted to the mystery of the Solar Star's disappearance. This anomaly pointed to a dimension beyond normal space. The friction plasma indicated the possible presence of an enormous energy applied to the space-time around the miner's craft. Could this have caused space to rupture and the craft to enter from one dimension to another? The big question: how did it coincide with our project and present path of the Andromeda?

We all stared at each other, speechless. After a moment's thought I regained my composure. "This cannot be a coincidence. I don't know how but something strange is at work here and my guess is it has to do with the strange object we discovered on the last day we saw the Solar Star."

Mickey's silky tone interrupted my thoughts. *'The propulsion system has cooled sufficiently for work to be carried out on the reactor, President Commander. I will initiate the refurbishing immediately.'*

"What are the chances of us not being able to make an effective repair?"

'I have no reservations about the repair, President Commander. The 3-D printer will be able to replicate the required parts. The reactor radiation-containment section will have to be strengthened to avert it being compromised on start-up. The system will be ready in another fourteen hours.'

Gary leaned back in his couch. "We will be slowing down at the appropriate time then?"

"It will add more time to our final arrival in the Pegasus constellation but cannot be helped now. Is contact with the Solar Star still on time as projected, Mickey?"

'Contact time is being recalculated as we speak, President Commander. The Solar Star is increasing its velocity, extending the contact time to four hours. If the increase continues it will eventually match our present speed again at the point of contact.'

The intrigue generated by this information caught my attention. It's almost as if the Solar Star wanted us to catch it. Could some foreign force have knowledge of our propulsion predicament? Perhaps an intelligent species more advanced than our own, in anticipation of all our movements?

Carla asked the obvious question. "Surely after seven months nobody could still be alive aboard the craft—it has no resources to sustain life beyond the short ferry trips."

"I would be inclined to agree with you, Hon. This is all very strange—we don't know what sort of intelligence we are dealing with here, only that it's very advanced."

The XO rubbed his chin. "I hope it's not an unfriendly one. It might be dangerous for us to approach the craft. Maybe we should leave it be, get our propulsion fixed and make the course change for the Great Square."

The Great Square of Pegasus, named for a neat configuration of four bright stars in the constellation, still remained a gargantuan fifty light years away.

Carla shot me a quick glance. "It took off with an entire shift of miners—does that seem friendly to you?"

The thought crossed my mind, but my curiosity got the better of me. "We owe it to the hundred and fifty-three miners to check this out. What if by some miracle, brought on by the oracle to whose power the Solar Star is subject, the miners are still alive?"

Carla and Gary both looked doubtful.

"We have four hours to decide but I, for one, am determined to get to the bottom of this mystery. We had written the vessel off months ago but there it is—right in front of us. We really cannot pass up the opportunity." I said.

The prospect of travel between the Andromeda and the Solar Star scared the shit out of me. The extreme compression of our craft at two-hundred and twenty-five thousand kilometers per second, posed the need for our emergency umbilical tunnel, which emitted the permeation of the stabilization force within the Andromeda to prevent us from being crushed. The circumstances provided a test for an untried system, which the experts assured me would work.

This would be an excellent opportunity to test it out. I would need to make a decision as to who might take the lead in the trip across—I believe I already knew. Carla would not support me in the decision but as far as I could see, there remained no other choice—it would have to be me.

"I need to talk to the NWERP representative. The decision to investigate affects everyone onboard the Andromeda."

Gary smiled at me. "Did you know the rep is a military appointment to the NWERP?"

This bit of news took me by surprise. "No—actually I didn't. Why would they need to send a military bot to do an administrative job?"

"Search me, Beckett. He wanted to introduce himself to us after release from the anti-acceleration pods but with all the drama I guess he decided to wait."

"It's strange Dr. Abrams didn't introduce him to us before the launch so we could see what we are dealing with."

Carla interjected with a theory. "I think they waited on purpose. The propulsion system is the military's latest baby—perhaps they wanted him to keep an eye on things."

Time constraints, compounded by the propulsion drama and the death of Brent Samuels, negated the opportunity for a one-on-one with the android representative, allocated to the project by Dr. Abrams. I needed to observe the standard protocol established for the android's presence and purpose in our midst. Any decision other than emergencies, which might jeopardize the project, would need to be discussed and ratified with the Andromeda City's representative.

"Mickey—please call the NWERP representative to the bridge—I've forgotten his name; is it Spackle?"

'His name is "Sparkle", President Commander—Lieutenant Sparkle, I believe.'

"Whatever—tell him it's urgent."

We turned our eyes back to the holo-platform. Due to the Andromeda's constant speed the image of the Solar Star appeared bigger than when first identified. My stomach felt a little queasy in consideration of what awaited us. At least knowing the fate of the missing miners would bring some closure to the incident of the craft's disappearance. Its reappearance did, however, pose a risky venture for the future of the project and I wondered how Lieutenant Sparkle would react to my decision.

Carla placed her arms around my waist and peered into my face. She possessed the most beautiful emerald-green eyes with crystal-clear, white sclera, one of the attractive characteristics responsible for my utter captivation when I first met her. She still is the most beautiful woman I have ever laid eyes on. I consider myself to be the luckiest of men to have caught her fancy—enough for her to accept my proposal of marriage.

The question I dreaded. "Have you decided on a boarding party yet?"

Her eyes held mine with intensity. She already knew my mind but needed me to voice it for the launch of her calculated trap—and I knew it.

"It has to be me, Darling. I don't want to put anyone else at risk if things go south."

"You're not considering going alone?"

"No—I'll take Happydoo and two of your security personnel with me. If anything happens and I don't return, you and Gary will be able to continue leading the project."

The emerald eyes burst into flame. "You are the most important member of this mission, Beckett. I won't allow you to go—if you refuse to listen then I insist on going with you."

I knew it would be hopeless to argue. She gets a look about her which signals real trouble when her mind is made up—there would be no compromises.

"This could be dangerous, Carla. I know you consider your past to qualify you as the most competent candidate for the risk but I don't want to put you in harm's way."

She pecked me on the lips in a complete dismissal of my misgivings. I suggest we take one of my deputies with us, Mike Hunter. He is the best I have in the security division.

I heard a noise behind me and turned to see the lieutenant, waiting for us to finish our conversation. Sparkle addressed me with the digital purr, common to Mickey and Happydoo, but with a deeper tone.

He saluted, a raise of the right-hand to the chest. *'I'm glad to finally get to meet you, President Commander.'*

He turned to Carla and bowed. *'—and this must be the lovely Mrs. Conroy.'*

Both Gary and I, taken a little by surprise by the android's shear charisma saluted in return, an instinctive reaction despite the fact we did not observe military protocols aboard the Andromeda, other than a short bow expected by subordinates.

"Yes—it's good to finally meet you, Lieutenant Sparkle."

∞∞

Eleven

The Lieutenant

'Is all well with the propulsion section, President Commander?'

"You have obviously heard what happened there, Sparkle. We managed to put the fire out and save the reactors, however, one is badly damaged and there are repairs to be made."

'I linked into Mickey's system in order to find out what happened. I understand there was a fatality?"

"Unfortunately, the fire moved very quickly to threaten the reactor area, causing the fire suppressant system to malfunction, leaving me no choice but to remove the breathable air. It is most regrettable that one of the four techs died."

'Yes, it's most unfortunate that human collateral damage occurred, however, it appears you saved the project from disaster, President Commander.'

"I would like to think so, Sparkle but losing a man is still a tragedy."

'It is to be expected, Sir. I understand that Mickey has identified a foreign craft in the space-time ahead of us.'

I told Sparkle about the Solar Star but he seemed to know all the details. I considered myself to be at a slight disadvantage—his ability to link into Mickey's system made all sorts of information available but androids have this capability—Happydoo could do the same.

'I believe you are considering boarding the vessel when we finally catch up with it, Sir.'

"I am—it will happen within the next four hours. Do you have any reservations, Sparkle."

'I do, President Commander. We do not know what intelligence has control of the Solar Star. It may be a trap.'

"Yes—that did cross my mind but I believe we cannot forgo the opportunity to discover what happened to those miners. Nor can we deny humanity's first known contact with an alien race."

'I must place it on record, President Commander—you are making a decision that might jeopardize the entire mission.'

"Your reservation is noted, Lieutenant. However, in the interests of the two reasons I've already mentioned, we will pursue the contact."

'Then I have only one more request, Sir.'

"And what would that be." I could feel my ire slowly rising. Was the android about to become confrontational?

'Consider taking me with you, President Commander.'

This request startled me. "I had actually planned to take my valet, Happydoo."

The lieutenant nodded. *'I understand but I ask you to consider my application, Sir. I possess the latest and most powerful quantum processor—the Diamond Series 1000. If you run into any type of trouble while on this mission, I will be your answer. My military and tactical abilities are far above anything your valet presently possesses. My eye-cameras are fitted with high-power lasers and can burn through three inches of steel.'*

The android made a good point but as it represented all the lay-people on our journey, 1165 of them, I entertained some ambivalence to his inclusion. Sparkle would be a real comfort to the people of Andromeda City in the event Carla and I did not make it back. Gary did a great job as the Ship's XO but his people's skills fell short. As for the Diamond Series processor, it eclipsed even Mickey's vast capability.

"Very well, Lieutenant—you've made yourself clear on the matter. I assume, as the NWERP rep you have someone who could fill in if we don't return?"

'I have deposited an upgrade-vile with the security purser. It contains a volume dealing with the logistics of the Habitat-replacement group and can be easily uploaded to Mickey's processor.'

"I understand. What exactly is it you are really on board for, Sparkle?"

I assume Dr. Abrams did not brief you on the full extent of my commission?'

"No, she didn't exactly tell me everything. I understood you would brief me on our first meeting—so...please feel free to explain your position—I'm listening."

If my words revealed a slight sarcasm, the lieutenant ignored it. *'Thank you, Sir. You are, of course, aware that my position as the NWERP representative is a military appointment, made by The Administration?"*

My dislike for The Administration stemmed from their totalitarian approach to Earth-wide rule. I did, however, consider the Andromeda and the NWERP mission, to be free from their big-brother approach tactics. This reflection may have been short-sighted.

'My main brief is to be a go-between for the crew of the Andromeda and the habitat-replacement group. Knowing how fickle the average human mind can become—excuse the intimation, I mean no disrespect—I am here to deal with any grievous considerations by the group should they arise.'

"Your words suggest there is still another part to your brief."

'We are going to experience the outworking of that other part through the boarding of the Solar Star and any other similar situations.'

"Have you been told to keep an eye on me and the decisions I make as the Commander of the mission?"

'I was told to offer you every bit of the vast capability of my processor and to support your decisions unless they obstruct the clear provisions of the NWERP charter and the objective of the mission.'

"Your military capability is purely for the protection of the mission?"

'Yes, it is, President Commander.'

"Anything else I should know, Sparkle?"

'Only that I should be consulted on anything to do with the propulsion system—there are anomalies that could arise under certain conditions not fully covered with the ship's propulsion engineers.'

"You are welcome to go through anything we do concerning the propulsion area, Lieutenant. When our repairs have been completed I would appreciate your input on the functionality of the system. God knows we might need it."

'Thank you, Sir.'

"That'll be all for now, Sparkle. I will call you one hour before we are due to board the Solar Star—we'll need to go over some things with Mickey."

The android came to attention, saluted and turned on its heel in true military style. Carla and Gary stared after Sparkle in astonishment as he left the bridge.

The XO found his tongue. "What the fuck is that?"

My mind whirled in a daze. "That, my friend, is going to be one of two things—a terrible nightmare, or a blessing in disguise."

"I think I understand why Mickey was not upgraded to the Diamond Series processor. The lieutenant will always hold the upper hand," said Carla.

I agreed. "I thought the Diamond Series 1000 still languished in the minds of tech visionaries."

"Its development certainly appears to have been kept a secret," said Gary.

Despite reservations about the Lieutenant's inclusion on the project more positives than negatives placated my embattled psyche. Any attempt by The Administration to enforce its will on my leadership, suffered one major drawback—with the distance from Earth, no realistic communication continuity of any sort existed. If the android's programs contained an aspect of investigation, there would be no way The Administration could influence Sparkle's reaction to any immediate situation. Should the lieutenant undermine my decisions, the entire project would be placed in jeopardy.

Mickey's silky voice broke the silence. 'We are one hour from point of contact with the Solar Star, President Commander.'

"Thank you Mickey—please summon Ensign Mike Hunter and Lieutenant Sparkle to the conference room. Carla and I will meet them there in five minutes.

I glanced at the holo-platform where the hologram of the Solar Star, now large and identifiable, hung in the darkness of space ahead and a shiver gripped my spine.

∞∞

Twelve

Boarding the Solar Star

Ensign Mike Hunter placed the code deactivator over the outer-hatch mechanism and jabbed at the input keys. The red light turned to green and the door slid open, accompanied by a rush of pressure from the emergency umbilical tube into the inner decompression chamber of the Solar Star. Carla, Lieutenant Sparkle and I waited for him to check out the inner-ship atmospheric information on the console, situated on the back of the inner door before entry to the ship. We wore EVA suits in the possible absence of breathable air within the craft.

Hunter gave a grunt of consent over the suit-intercom and moved into the entrance portal of the ship. We stepped in behind him and the inner door snapped shut. The Solar Star appeared to have power to all entrance and exit hatches. The ensign turned and undid the clasp on his helmet to indicate the presence of breathable air and everyone followed suite. I looked around in wonder at the portico area. All appeared as it should be.

The ferry could accommodate two hundred people in its main passenger section, closed off by the double doors in front of us. Each door possessed a tiny window, through which the green-glow of a misty vapor could be seen. This struck me as odd.

"I don't recall any system employed on the ferries which emits such a greenish glow."

Lieutenant Sparkle moved to one of the windows. 'The vapor is of a cryogenic nature, President Commander. The green glow is an unknown but the atmosphere beyond the doors is breathable.'

Carla broke her silence. "Is it safe for us to enter?"

'It appears to be safe, Mrs. Conroy.'

I activated the door mechanism and the two doors slid open to reveal an extraordinary sight. We all stared, speechless for several moments before I found my voice.

"What the—."

'It looks like someone—something—has placed the entire crew into a hibernation process of some sort, President Commander.'

The bulk of the seats in the section supported flexible, pod-like bags which contained a mixture of a vapor and a liquid. The unmistakable solid content in each pod followed the contours of a human form. "So this is what happened to the missing miners." I mused.

"Are they alive?" Mike Hunter stepped over to the closest pod to jab at it with his laser weapon.

The pod material absorbed the prod and popped back to its original shape.

My intrigue grew by the second. "It would appear so. The pods are obviously life support systems, similar to our own in the Andromeda."

"But who, what—." Carla could not tear her eyes from the pods, each with its own incandescent glow.

Before anyone could answer her question a loud hum penetrated the entire ship and the liquid, vapor mixture in the pods, agitated and bubbled. We fell silent as the glow in the room increased in intensity. Mike Hunter raised his laser in readiness. The pods, not attached to any sort of unitary feed system or connection of tubes appeared to be isolated units. Each received power from a source within the ship. I looked around with alarm but saw no solution to the mystery. There appeared to be no particular source of power or collective control equipment. The hum died to an audible murmur and the agitation of the pod contents abated.

"Do not be afraid. I mean you no harm."

The voice came from everywhere in the room, each word with deliberate articulation. We glanced around and at each other. Carla grabbed my arm in fright and Mike Hunter turned to stare out of the double doors at no one in particular, his weapon pointed in the direction of the entrance hatch. Sparkle retained complete composure.

"Who are you? Where are you?" I asked.

"My name is Ossimantus."

Again, the clearness and articulation of the words impressed us.

"I am situated within the Orbitron which you will find on the vessel's flight deck."

The flight deck, hidden by another set of doors at the far-end of the passenger section, still awaited our scrutiny.

"Orbitron? What's that?"

"It is the foreign object your mining crew found on the asteroid you call Tiffany."

"Where are you from?" I asked.

The voice softened. "I suggest we get more acquainted before I tell you about myself—please do not be afraid—come to the bridge. I need to prepare you for our meeting."

We looked at each other. Carla and Hunter registered traces of fear on their faces. Carla whispered to me, "Beckett—I'm scared."

I whispered back. "It hasn't tried to harm us yet. What do we have to lose?"

'I am registering a life-form on the bridge, President Commander.'

"You and Carla stand by, Sparkle. Ensign Hunter and I will approach the bridge."

Hunter and I moved along the rows of seats toward the double doors on the far side of the passenger area. The doors swung open on approach and scared me shitless. We froze in the doorway.

"Please step onto the bridge. There is nothing to fear," the voice assured us.

I could see the object perched on the ground between us and the main flight console. The same greenish glow emitted from the pods emanated from it, enough to light the vessel's main control panel.

We edged into the room. Hunter held the laser at waist height, pointed at the object. We paused about eight feet from the Orbitron.

"I am going to make an appearance. Please stay calm—place your weapon on the floor—if you comply with my request no one will get hurt."

Hunter looked across at me and I nodded. He slowly placed the laser on the floor in front of him.

The glow of light from the Orbitron brightened and the atmosphere around it thickened into a cloud of green. We waited, breathless and afraid. A creature slid through the wall of the object and stood still. I gaped; Hunter remained speechless and Carla gasped, with hands clasped to her cheeks and eyes as round as saucers. We all stood frozen to the spot and stared at the apparition in front of us.

The creature's single eye scanned each one of us. About four feet tall and transparent, the alien's body looked like a large condom. Through the transparency of its outer skin, forms and shapes of innards could be seen; two short, arm-like protuberances extended from each side and brandished stubby, three-fingered hands. The face, if it could be so called, contained no nose or chin and a slit where a mouth would be on a human, figured into the strange mix of features. No legs protruded from the convex lower shape—it seemed to float several inches off the ground, like a ghost.

A holo-movie presentation of such a crea-ture would have me in a fit of laughter but instead, I gawped. Out of the corner of my eye I could see the others on the ogle in a similar fashion.

Then it spoke. "I also stared at your species when I first laid an eye on it. You humans have so much definition about your bodies—I'm afraid you'll find me plain and shapeless."

After a moment I found my tongue. "You seem to be acquainted with our...species. I assume the miners, all in apparent hibernation, are the first specimens you saw?"

"On the contrary, Commander Conroy—my kind have been acquainted with your species for the entire duration of your evolution."

The alien knew my name—at a guess, in-formation gleaned from the miners.

"Why did you hijack the Solar Star, Mr.—."

"—Ossimantus. I had no option at the time but to take the Orbitron back to the dimension from whence I came. I apologize if this caused you some trouble, Commander. I had every intention of bringing them all back. The truth is my Orbitron, having been compromised, had been stuck in your dimension for far too long and I needed to return to confirm its repair."

"Where is this dimension?"

"A complicated concept for one who has never been exposed to our physics Commander—let's call it another realm, running in conjunction with your space-time. The two can only merge with the intervention of, what is for you an infinite amount of energy, but for us it's a common factor of our local production."

"What do you call your species and your home?"

The creature hesitated for a moment. "The best translation from my tongue to yours would resemble *Lumbrians*. The world from which we originate would similarly be called *Translumbria*."

My mental capacity approached overload. "You are saying you do not originate from within our universe. What is your reason for being here?"

"Your universe was seeded from our domain. Another challenging concept for your philosophical approaches and understanding of physics —my mandate is to monitor the progress of your species."

Carla overcame her verbal inertia. "You caused the Big Bang?"

"There is so much for us to discuss, Mrs. Conroy but now is not the right time for it. May I suggest we awaken all your miners and get them transferred back to your ship?   Then I'll transfer myself and the Orbitron. It will be my pleasure to share as much as I can with you and the Commander.   My real mission is to help you complete your project—there is much danger ahead."

∞∞

THIRTEEN

Ossimantus

The twelve hours which followed turned out to be a busy period for Carla and I. De-hibernation of the miners took most of this time, the process turned out to be the same as we would have followed on the Andromeda with our own, still to be executed, process.

Our guest possessed all the knowledge of human-hibernation science needed for long durations in space and pointed out some aspects of the process we could improve aboard the Andromeda. The miner's sojourn of seven months in the Lumbrian dimension passed as in the blink of an eye for them and no one retained any knowledge of the duration. The shift boss, James Carter, relayed how they, in the process of departure from Tiffany, witnessed their surround fade into darkness. The sudden revival from the hibernation process, on our visit to the Solar Star, left them even more confused as to how we appeared on the scene. I spent half-an-hour in explanation of the reality of their rescue; several of the miners refused to believe it. It would take several days for the idea of their new situation to sink in—the fact none of them would ever see Earth again and the process of habitat relocation, required some urgent examination. Councilors helped with debrief and it would be a matter of time before they could be absorbed into the day-to-day operations aboard the Andromeda.

Ossimantus remained in the Solar Star until the four of us plus all the miners, made it safely back through the umbilical tunnel, to the Andromeda. The creature assured me it would follow—the outer-hatch and the tunnel provided enough area to accommodate the Orbitron and we cast several backward glances of fascination as the object followed on behind us. The Alien informed us the tunnel would not be necessary for its transfer but it would use it in the interests of energy conservation.

On completion of the transfer I gave Mickey the order to withdraw the umbilical tunnel and the Solar Star to be cut loose. It would continue to coast through space at its present speed until the gravity of some distant star pulled the empty vessel into an orbit and eventual obliteration. The course of the Andromeda altered under Mickey's astute control, to pursue a new trajectory toward the Pegasus constellation.

With the Orbitron stored in the cargo-hold, one level below our living-quarters we arranged a meeting with Gary Pearson and our executive fight staff for formal introduction. A stunned silence followed the creature's entrance to the boardroom.

I made the introduction and couldn't help stifle a laugh at the expense of the senior crew members. Their faces presented a uniform picture of astonishment. Ossimantus bobbed in acknowledgement at my explanation of our first face-to-face on the Solar Star.

I asked the alien to address us with regard to future concerns.

"I understand this is much harder for you to absorb than for me. As I told the President Commander, my species has been well acquainted with yours for millions of Earth years and it's why I am ofay with your customs and language."

You could have heard a pin drop each time the alien paused in its story. Everyone's eyes became riveted on the creature as it confirmed many of our evolutionary events—the initiation of our universe or 'spawning', through a process of dimensional propagation. Ossimantus alluded to other similar initiations throughout many different dimensions—other universes, both similar and different to ours. The explanation of the Earth's evolution, matched our fossil records and confirmed the five great extinction events, the rise of humankind and journey to present status.

"The sixth extinction event is a combination of three major calamities brought on by human disregard for the planet, the cycles performed by orbital phenomenon, which resulted in loss of the magnetic field protection and as you have learned, the approach of a dangerous neutron star to the solar system. Lumbrians knew such a time would come."

I instructed everyone present, due to the many possible enquiries, Carla, Gary and I would ask questions.

Carla waved her hand in the air to catch the alien's attention. "Do Lumbrians, having spawned a universe, not have the power to change things at will?"

"Unfortunately not, Mrs. Conroy. The universe is very much in charge of itself and once spawned will take on a nature as directed by the great mysterious force, or forces which occupy the energy. We actually know very little about the real power behind everything. I can only anticipate the future outworking according the natural laws—much like yourselves."

Gary intervened. "So...you aren't like a god or a deity who knows all things?"

"Definitely not, Lieutenant Commander—we, like yourselves, evolved with some differences in a similar fashion, also subject to much philosophical meandering. We have, however, the benefit of eons of knowledge passed down from generation to generation. Our lifespans are much longer than yours."

I asked the next most logical question. "How long do you live for?"

Ossimantus reflected on the question for a moment. "A typical Lumbrian would live for fifty-million of your Earth years and then it's only the consciousness that passes on—the body is simply the carrier of the mind and will continue receiving a new conscious entity, for as long as our civilization lasts. We have an accumulated history, the equivalent of 60 Billion Earth years, in the Translumbrian dimension."

Gary's curiosity got the better of him. "How strange this is for us—the body doesn't die but the consciousness passes on. What causes this change and where does the consciousness go?"

The alien snorted which may have been the equivalent of a laugh. "I understand your quandary, Lieutenant Commander. Please remember the Translumbrian dimension is very different to yours. We do not know why the consciousness suddenly decides to pass on or where it goes to—if it goes anywhere at all or simply ceases to exist."

It seemed obvious to me the Lumbrians found themselves in the same position as we, in regard to their immortality. More important things needed to be discussed so I changed the subject.

"You mentioned there would be dangers ahead for our project—what exactly do you foresee and how do we avoid these future hazards?"

The alien bobbed several times. I took it to be the equivalent of the human nod of the head.

"You will not be able to avoid the problems, however, you will at least be able to prepare yourselves—but even so, it will still be very dangerous."

The statement did not surprise me but the alien's prior knowledge of potential future perils would be a great heads-up. "Please, tell us what you know."

Ossimantus gazed around at all the expectant faces and bobbed again, slower this time, and revealed a reluctance to impart the information.

"There has been an intrusion from another dimension we call Crusta. These aliens have also seeded several domains, similar to yours—they are seeking to gain control of Translumbrian seeding and subjugate species in your universe, to spread their influence. We have been at war with them for a long time."

The creature paused to allow the words to sink in. A cold shiver raced along my spine. The information confirmed the theories humankind has promulgated for hundreds of years—we are not alone in the universe. The silence in the room became palpable as Ossimantus continued.

"The Crustans are beings who thrive on power and tyranny. Their entire social structure is built on war and enmity with anyone who opposes their will. The race is singular in anatomical makeup and is ruled by a tyrant king who has control telepathically with all subjects. They pose a severe threat to all species in your universe."

This news brought me little comfort. We faced a mammoth task in the location of a new home. To face an advanced, warlike group of aliens, tipped the scales out of our favor.

Carla flung her hand in the air. "You are confirming the presence of many other species in our universe—do you know how many there are?"

Ossimantus stared at her with his one eye and bobbed. "You are aware there are over one hundred billion star groups you humans call galaxies, making the number of habitable bodies, to number in the trillions. The truth is we don't know how many different species there are because we do not have the resources to monitor them all."

My concern still lay with the Crustans. "Being astute enough to monitor the event which gave rise to our project you will also know why we are in need of finding a new home for the human species —do you know where the Crustans are at this time?"

The question received a different alien expression which sounded like the escape of compressed air. "I only know they are close to the vicinity of the Pegasus Constellation."

"Are the Lumbrians able to assist us in the event of a confrontation with these creatures?"

The alien made the same air sound. "I am afraid the only help we are able to render is the advice I am able to give you. Translumbria is in a protracted war with Crusta and our conventional forces are fully extended in our own dimension, however, the Crustans have some fatal weaknesses and flaws which I will help you to exploit."

His words brought some relief to my fragile state of mind and I knew we still needed answers to many quandaries but the on-duty ensign, in charge of the main console, interrupted.

"President Commander, please come quickly to the bridge."

∞∞

Fourteen

Trouble In The Ranks

About thirty people crowded into the bridge area. They stood with folded arms and sullen expressions of hostility. Lieutenant Sparkle stood to one side, a frown creased his synthetic skin and I assumed there to be trouble in the ranks.

"What's this all about, Sparkle?"

The android turned away from the crowd to address me. *'Some of the folk are not happy about your recent decisions, President Commander. They have asked me to represent them by putting a suggestion to you.'*

My hackles rose. "I see. What decisions are we referring to, Sparkle?"

'First of all, your decision to remove all the breathable air from the reactor chamber—doing so cost a life. They have been speaking to the fission techs, one who feels it was not a necessary action in order to deal with the fire hazard.'

I could see the woman, Laura Samuels among the group of dissenters. The lieutenant continued.

'The second decision they questioned is the allowing of an alien presence aboard the ship.

There is no knowing what motive the creature might have. The abduction of the Solar Star appears very much like a hostile act to them.'

"What suggestion are they wanting to bring forward, Lieutenant?"

'It is suggested we move to a more democratic process for the making of decisions that might endanger the ship's compliment. They feel the Andromeda is more like a small city and could do with the wisdom of a committee in the major decision-making process—that the nature and complexity of demands on such leadership should not be vested in one person.'

The request challenged my leadership integrity and for a few moments my ego got the better of me. Then in retrospect it struck me; their response, born out of fear and ignorance, required a diplomatic approach. As their leader it would be expedient to win their confidence—they needed a leader whom they could trust. Years ago I would have reacted in a different way. Conroy senior, in the neglect of his parental responsibilities, raised an insecure rebel of a son who suffered through much of his young adult life with a strong sense of rejection—until circumstances forced a maturity. I did not wish to rehash old habits again.

"May I address the group?"

The Lieutenant acquiesced and turned to face the rebels while my mind raced to find the correct words to put them at ease.

"I understand perfectly where your fears regarding my leadership are coming from. The idea of a more democratic decision-making process is good one. I can absolutely agree there is wisdom in a multitude of counselors."

I saw Laura Samuels shift her position from folded arms to a more open stance.

"The problem with certain decisions, however, is the speed with which they sometimes need to be made. In the case of the fire and removal of breathable air in the ship's nuclear chamber it may seem debatable, but the fire reached a critical point—the reactor was seconds away from blowing up. This would have definitely ended our project."

Their faces, like masks of wax gave no indication of acknowledgment of the difficulty, or merit to my argument.

"The XO and the Master computer both ratified my decision. There was no time to consult anyone else. Regarding the alien creature in our midst, I again counselled with the XO, my wife, Carla, and your lieutenant Sparkle—neither questioned my decision to bring it on board—in fact this might be the best decision I have ever made."

Turning back to Sparkle I encouraged him to support my words. The android hesitated for a moment then turned to face the dissenters again.

'I find myself in agreement with the President Commander regarding the fire incident. I do feel, however, that bringing the alien aboard is

questionable. I was not included in the conference with the creature in the boardroom so I can't really assess the situation.'

Sparkle made a good point. I understood what motivated his answer and moved to rectify the perception.

"Please forgive my lack of protocol. The lieutenant is the people's representative on the project and I should have remembered to include him in the introduction of our guest. There will be more interview time with the alien. I invite a representative delegation from your group to attend these."

Not convinced the dissenters looked around at each other. It would be imperative for me to set a strong foundation to gain their cooperation in future issues. I did not need their continued opposition to my leadership; a little leaven leavens the whole lump.

Sparkle further eased the atmosphere. *'If you good folk would remember the lectures we all received from Dr. Abrams before signing up for this quest: the final say in all things will remain in the President Commander's hands. While we welcome good suggestions on the many matters of public protocol, accountability for the project lies with him. We have only started our journey and I'm sure our leader will prove to all of us, in time, he deserves our trust.'*

A few members of the group appeared to be in agreement. Others looked a little undecided. Laura Samuels stared at the floor—if she agreed with Sparkle's explanation, it did not show.

I made one further comment in an attempt to end the deadlock. "We have been able to rescue one hundred and fifty-three miners, a feat, I'm sure, gratifies everyone. The miners are extremely grateful to be back with their own—the alien made this possible. I am sure it will tell us why the apparent abduction happened in the first place. "

'I will organize a delegation from the ship's secular community, President Commander. We look forward to meeting with Ossimantus at your earliest convenience,' said Sparkle.

The group seemed to have been placated and after a few stares aimed at the bridge in general they moved off toward the verticap. Laura Samuels would not look me in the eye as she passed by and I knew the death of her husband still posed a barrier to my leadership. I could understand her reluctance to let it be—maybe, in time her hurt would heal and allow her to accept the status quo.

Gary Pearson arrived at the bridge after the interview and saw the last members of the group step into the verticap. I explained the situation.

The XO ran a hand through his mousy-brown, short hair. "I had an idea Laura Samuels might be talking to others about the circumstances under which her husband died. It's a good thing Sparkle was asked to be the spokesperson—being a military bot, would give him a good insight into leadership dynamics."

*

At the end of the shift Carla and I decided to retire to our quarters. The busy twelve hours left us both drained of energy. The discovery of the lost miners and an alien, plus some realistic facts about our universe, all compounded by the delegation of dissenters, added sufficient strain to the concerns we already carried.

Carla, not ready to relinquish her mind's hold on the enormity of these factors turned to me with sleepy eyes. "Do you think Laura Samuels intends to cause trouble for us, hon?"

"It's hard to say, sweetheart but let's allow things to work out in the most natural way possible. Right now I have only a small amount of energy left—energy I would like to expend with you. I have other activities in mind which do not include talking about the present problems. We'll face them on the morrow."

She pulled me close to her body and draped a leg over my thigh. Within seconds we entered the world of physical and mental intimacy where all problems disappear and libidos rise.

∞∞

Fifteen

The First Hibernation

Seven years later with the approach of the first seven year hibernation period, group B prepared for hyper-sleep and consciousness transition. Gary Pearson, our executive office, would be the most senior ranked flight crew member to take part in this event. Once his hyper-sleep period ended he would take over from me, assisted by my personal valet, Happydoo, at which time Carla and I would enter hibernation with group A.

"Are you ready for this, Gary?"

"As ready as I will ever be, Beckett. I keep reminding myself—this has never been done for such a long period before, however, the tests done in the labs on Earth proved flawless."

"We eagerly await your return. The interesting aspect of the lab tests showed little aging in the human body during hibernation. The tests had only been done over a year's duration so we would hope for the same result after completion of the seven-year period, but it remains to be seen."

The XO smiled. "My group will go down in history, one way or the other. Of course, if it's true, then you will be technically catching me up in age."

We both laughed as Gary stepped into the hibernation pod. The hyper-sleep technicians fussed over the connections of various life-support systems and tubes. They checked all the XO's vitals and then placed a facial mask over his nose and mouth. The entrance cover closed to seal him in and his eyes searched for mine, as the life support liquid filled the pod. A change to our system came at the Alien's suggestion of a special additive to the amniotic fluid, present in each container. The additive came from a substance, unknown to us but common to the Lumbrian Dimension of elements, which caused the green glow we first witnessed aboard the Solar Star. Ossimantus assured us the combination would preserve the human bodies in perfect stasis.

I saluted Gary as the liquid engulfed him and received the glimmer of a response in return, before his eyes closed and the clock above commenced the time-duration count. It would be seven years before Gary Pearson again walked the decks of the Andromeda. In my heart I wished him well.

Seven hundred souls would follow suit over a two-week period to account for the entirety of group B. The remainder of the ships company, group A, continued on with their lives while Mickey monitored the hibernation process. I turned and walked on unsteady legs toward the verticap, on route to the bridge, with emotions awry.

Carla stared at the holo-platform which provided us with a view of the space ahead of us. "How did it go, Hon?"

"All appears to be well—so far. It's a really weird feeling to see one of your friends being swallowed up by that green fluid," I said.

"Don't worry, Sweetheart. Ozzy said it would all be fine and he should know."

Over time Ossimantus, the alien, became a firm friend and confidant. We shortened his name to "Ozzy" and spent many months, after our initial meeting, to glean wonderful truths about our cosmos—we developed an insatiable need to know more. Sone concepts we could not fathom and the science involved left our limited earth-bound intelligence, strained to the limits. When I pressed for more explanation he would say, "All in good time, Beckett—all in good time.

"I see by the con distance holo-indicator we have now surpassed 5.2 light years distance from Earth," mused Carla.

"It's mind-boggling when you try to think in terms of kilometers—fifty trillion, give or take a few."

Carla leaned her head on my shoulder. "Yet, we are only one tenth of the distance to Pegasus.

When did Ozzy say he would visit with us again?—
I really miss him."

After his initial stay with us Ozzy left,
promised to return for short periods in each year
of space flight, until we reached our final destination. This would prove important to us because of
news gleaned from his dimension in regard to the
Crustans. The alien assured me we would be instructed on ways to approach contact with the war-
mongers, once closer to the Pegasus constellation.

"He should be due quite soon—Happydoo
will know exactly when that is."

The Andromeda ran all its systems on Earth
Dynamical Time. We observed days, weeks,
months and years for the sake of living life in sync
with the accustomed Earth-cycle of our minds and
bodies. The atomic clocks, however, took the time
dilation aspect into account. For every year passed
by on our ill-fated home planet, .585 of a year
passed onboard the Andromeda, a weird concept
to grasp. Two time pieces existed side by side on
the bridge—one kept Earth Dynamical time and
the other, dilated time.

Once we found the exoplanet, 51 Peg d, we
would customize time to the local dynamical system and suffer the transition. The star, 51 Pegasi,
replicated our sun in many respects and the planet, one of several but the most Earth-like, orbited
at a distance of 155 million kilometers, on average.

"Did you ever ask him why it would not be possible for us to have him pull a 'Solar Star' trick with the Andromeda and whisk us through his dimension to Pegasus—if it were possible we could cut out the time duration and all those horrible hibernations."

I gave her full marks for thinking of the concept. "I did ask him about it, hon. He said the Translumbrian dimension was infinitely bigger than our own and even at the speeds they are able to travel it would still take us about the same length of time. I'm afraid we're stuck with the distance and the hibernations."

She gave me a crestfallen look and nuzzled her nose into my neck. "Can we be together in a pod during hyper-sleep?"

I laughed. "Unfortunately they didn't think of dual occupancy pods, Sweetheart. You'll have to tough it out on your own."

*

Three weeks later, Gary's counterpart, Space-Captain Peter Manning, approached the main con where I busily scanned through the hibernation pod holo-file for group B, to check on all the life support systems responsible for the lives of the hyper-sleepers.

"President Commander—your valet asked if he could talk to you in private. He is in the cargo hold getting the Orbitron area ready for the alien's visit. He asked if your neuro-transmitter was working."

My temple-contact pad lay on the desk in my quarters. Due to the wealth of communication facilities aboard, it is seldom needed and many a-shift I neglected to wear it. "No problem Peter. I'll go to the hold and talk with him."

Several minutes later the verticap dropped me off in the cargo hold, a huge open area, for the storage of raw materials. Happydoo sat astride a large crate with one finger connected to an input panel, located on a steel support pillar—his processor linked to one of Mickey's many monitoring-terminals. These terminals link to the many facets of the Andromeda's life support systems and all executive crew members have access.

'Greetings, Master Beckett. I'm sorry to trouble you but I've discovered a strange irregularity and I wanted you to be the first to know about it.'

∞∞

Sixteen

A Fortuitous Discovery

"What have you discovered, Happydoo?"

'It was quite by accident, Master Beckett. I wanted to check the exact dates of all the hibernation periods for the purpose of knowing who would be in command of the main console during the alien's future visits.'

"If I remember, Ozzy committed the times of future visits to you. Why would it be of any importance who commanded the con?"

'I'm not sure why, Master Beckett but the alien wanted to know—I assume he had his own reasons and I promised I would supply the information on the next visit. With that event taking place within the coming week I felt it expedient to start the preparation of the Orbitron's resting area today. While checking the hibernation period dates I came across a strange anomaly.'

"By anomaly do you mean a break from protocol or a mistake in calculation of settings?"

'The anomaly exposes a break in protocol which indicates a change of particular settings on one of the pods during the next hibernation peri-

od. It has been made to look as though it was a miscalculation.'

"How do you know it wasn't an error?"

'Because errors are picked up by Mickey's monitoring programs, Master Beckett—if, however, a protocol, upon which a computation is based, has been purposefully changed no error will be reflected.'

Happydoo's processor contained detailed information of all algorithmic computation in control of the systems aboard the Andromeda, a total eclipse of my limited knowledge. "Do you mean a certain command for something—like, turn on or shut off?"

'Yes, Master Beckett. I am Happy to say you have hit the nail on the head. Two pods involved in the second hibernation period have this anomaly. One protocol in their operation has been altered to drain the amniotic fluid prematurely plus cancel the ensuing alarm. The lives within these two pods would immediately end. Both sets of consciousness vials have also been altered to terminate at the same time.'

I stared at the android in astonishment. When my composure returned I asked the next obvious question. "To whom are these two pods allocated?"

Happydoo hesitated for a moment. *'You and Miss Carla, Master Beckett.'*

"Someone has deliberately tampered with our pod's protocols in order to eliminate us?"

'It would seem so, Master Beckett. I have communicated with Mickey regarding the incident but the protocols were already in place when Mickey's processor was programmed at the NWE base. The error diagnostics, run after the initial programming, did not pick up the change because technically there was no error.'

I did not understand this reason, however, it didn't alter the fact—someone altered the original program to have Carla and myself, eliminated from the project.

"Is there any way of knowing who might have done this, Happydoo"

'I'm afraid not, Master Beckett. It could be any number of people who might have had access during the refurbishing of the Andromeda. I have obviously instructed Mickey to redo the protocol and change the outcome.'

I could have hugged the android but response to such gestures are not a part of the general program and he would not have been able to appreciate it.

"I owe you my life, Happydoo—Miss Carla's too. IF you hadn't had a reason to *check* the hibernation periods this might never have come to light."

Happydoo initiated his famous foot-stomp routine. *'I am happy to do it, Master Beckett, but in all truth it is the alien you should thank. His request led me to the anomaly.'*

*

"Carla's eyes containing a glimmer of fear. "Someone tried to have us eliminated?"

My compulsion to withhold the information from her seemed wise at first, but then I knew the truth would surface sooner or later. As head of Andromeda's security, the matter would come under her investigation and bring it to her attention.

"Take it easy, Honey. Mickey has revised the protocols so the danger is averted for the time being. We need to do some investigation on who might want us dead and does it still represent a future threat."

"My immediate thought would have been Laura Samuels but if this plan was already in place before we left Earth it would rule her out. What about Lieutenant Sparkle?" She said.

"Sparkle came in as a late inclusion, long after the programming of the systems. He never came near the Andromeda until we were ready to launch and I doubt it could have been Dr. Abrams —what motive could she possibly have had?"

Carla finger-twirled a strand of blonde hair. "I'll spend some time going through all the personnel records. I may be able to come up with something but life is going to be a bit tense for us until it's sorted out."

I looked doubtful. "You'll have to check for anyone who might have had access during the refurbishing phase plus who might have had a motive—it will be like looking for a needle in a haystack."

"I realize that, Beckett."

I could sense the irritation in her tone. She would know the enormity of such a process better than I.

"Sorry, hon. I didn't mean—

"It's Okay, Sweetheart. Leave it to me—I'll work out a way of systematically coming to a conclusion. It's what I was trained to do in the Intelligence Agency."

I pecked her on the cheek and headed for safer ground—the bridge. Happydoo would be a great help in her quest and I determined to solicit his assistance at the earliest convenience. The possibility of collusion, between someone involved with the refurbish program and a crew member, now amongst us on the Andromeda, ranked high on my list of concerns. I knew it would be best left to Carla to sort the matter out—my attention and focus needed to be on the day-to-day oversight of the ship.

*

"I bring you greetings from Translumbria, President Commander."

Ozzy's arrival in the Orbitron created a stir with the ship's population. Our one local news provider on board, "Galaxy News", featured the visit—a full week ahead of the alien's arrival—one could say, aboard the Andromeda, Ozzy occupied the honor imposed upon a celebrity.

"It's good to see you again, Ozzy. I trust you had a pleasant trip."

"I certainly did—how is Carla?"

"She is very well, thank you—busy with a special project."

With the Orbitron parked in its area Ozzy, happy to be back amongst friends, bobbed along next to me on route to the vericap. In the board-room, I engaged the entrance force-field to ensure our privacy.

"Your XO, Gary Pearson is now in hiberna-tion, I believe."

"Yes, the process went well and the new amniotic fluid is proving to be an excellent medi-um for life support. Happydoo told me you asked him for the hibernation dates of the two groups. I would be interested to know why you needed the information?"

Ozzy looked a little puzzled. "Oh yes, I re-member now. I wanted to plan my arrivals to coin-cide with those dates. It is expedient to visit the ship soon after one of the commanders goes into hyper-sleep—your hibernation in particular—in case there might be something of importance for me to know."

I smiled. "I am so glad you did."

The story of Happydoo's fortuitous discovery followed. The alien, with an occasional bob of the head, remained silent.

"This must be very distressing for you and Carla. I hope something comes to light soon. At least you have nothing to worry about for the next seven years—if the perpetrator, or an accomplice is on board, they aren't going to try anything during the next seven years."

Ozzy made sense. My mind, focused on the "who", did not take this truth into consideration. With the evil deed planned for the middle of group A's hyper-sleep period, the perpetrator could be relaxed and not know about the scheme's detection. This gave us time to work on a plan to expose of our enemy.

The alien swayed from side to side—an action which perhaps meant a mixture of joy and mirth, and with quick intake-of-air sounds, bobbed several times. He enjoyed those moments, when the scales fell from my eyes.

"Now my dear friend, I have something of importance to share with you. Our Lumbrian scouts, who monitor the entrances and exits from your universe, have assured me the Crustans are making inroads to the area where you are headed."

I stiffened. "Are we talking about the general constellation or specific stars?"

Ozzy held my stare with his single eye. "Specific—the area of 51 Pegasus."

∞∞

Seventeen

Searching for a Culprit

51 Pegasus is a yellow-orange, main sequence star, luminosity type G4 to 5 and is similar to our sun. Several planets orbited the star, with 51 Peg d the focal point of our attention. At 160 million kilometers it is in the goldilocks area for habitability and can be seen through Sky-eye three, Earth's largest space-based telescope. Water and vegetation are present but intelligent life still remains unconfirmed. Our cosmologists believe the planet contains an atmosphere but do not guarantee it to be breathable. We have called our soon-to-be new home, "Hera-Soter", after the wife of Zeus and the ancient Greek word for savior.

"How much do you know about 51 Peg d?"

Ozzy bobbed once and ogled me. "Not much more than you do, I'm afraid. There are many habitable planets in your universe I have not been able to explore—it's not my purpose to do so. We have kept an eye on a few civilizations, yours being one of them, to prevent creatures like the Crustans from interfering with progress."

"I remember you mentioning the abundance of life in our universe but are there any other civilizations like ours?"

"There are over a thousand, spread out over one hundred prominent galaxies, of which we have made contact with."

"Are these civilizations more advanced than we are?"

"Only a few are more advanced than humankind. Many are still in the early stages of their evolution."

"Do you think the Crustans got lucky when they chose the area we are heading for?"

"I believe it to be a coincidence. There is a dimension portal close to your Pegasus constellation being used by the Crustans to enter and exit the universe—they might have noticed the possibilities of your Hera-Soter planet."

"Are they similar to us—do they breathe air?"

"The Crustan dimension supports many aquatic worlds, making their primary need a water solution that supports a certain percentage of oxygen. They are able to sustain life in a heavily waterlogged, humid type atmosphere for short periods but basically need to be in water for better quality living. That might be one of the reasons they are in the Pegasus area. There are many planets containing oceans of water."

"Is their reason for invading our domain the need to find new resources like water?"

The Alien weaved and sucked air for a moment. "I believe they are short on resources but this is not the real reason for an invasion. Their entire philosophy of life is constructed around war. War is the prime reason for anything in Crusta. The Crustans will defeat a civilization just because they can—then kill off the conquered just for sport."

"They sound like a very violent species," I said.

Ozzy bobbed several times. "They are quite formidable in battle and you will want to avoid them at all costs."

It appeared we teetered between a rock and hard place. "How are we supposed to inhabit Hera-Soter without making contact with these beasts?"

"That is something we will have time to figure out, my friend."

*

While I bombarded our alien friend with more questions Carla took off to further our quest for the exposition of the potential murderer. Happydoo spent a great deal of time on the relocation project's records. Our initial contract plus the refurbish records of the Andromeda, took special priority. Mickey's vast memory contained every request, decision made and action undertaken, throughout our initial training period—Carla's intense scrutiny of all the details would take a long time.

She discovered some resistance to our appointment in the minutes of one of the many meetings between Dr. Abrams and The Administration. A certain trustee, an android named Quon, voiced his disagreement to my leadership of the venture but it didn't raise a flag for me; several people agreed an android might be the better choice. The suggestion never even gained the floor as a motion so I discounted the notion of any complicity on his part to oust me.

Carla immediately asked Happydoo to seek for a link between Quon and Lieutenant Sparkle but it produced no intent on behalf of either android. Another clue surfaced, however, to establish a possible intrusion to one of the restricted areas of the Andromeda—installation of the bridge instrumentation. This clue served as a possible opportunity for the hibernation procedure algorithms to have been altered.

Ozzy decided to retire to the Orbitron for a period of time and left me free to seek out Carla.

I found her and Happydoo in examination of a holo-file on the desk viewing-platform in my office. "You two look animated—anything new?"

Carla continued her scrutiny. "I believe we may have something. No identity as yet but a definite intrusion to a restricted area by someone who didn't have clearance."

"How could anyone manage that?"

"It must have been difficult but I'll let Happydoo explain—he discovered it."

'It took place during a mandatory drill, Master Beckett. You will remember the regular training we all received on fire control.'

"Yes, of course. It's a time of my life I will never forget."

'Everyone had to attend—it was the only time when all other functions ceased. I discovered a sign-in to the Master Computer Center—the main-frame chamber where Mickey's processor is situated, Master Beckett—a particle-bit chip was removed and then replaced.'

"Let me guess—the chip containing the hibernation protocols."

'That's correct, Master Beckett.'

"But, there is no identity on the sign-in. How would that even be possible?"

Carla provided a possible answer. "The contractor who installed the sign-in system could have created some sort of back door."

This lead appeared to be productive. My concern, however, rested in the extent to which Mickey's collateral knowledge contained detailed information of the companies, chosen to refurbish the spacecraft. The files, offered by the contractors, might contain basic details about their personnel. This type of information depended on the thoroughness of Dr. Abrams and her human resource departments over the contractor adjudication process.

"Assuming you're correct about a backdoor being created in the system, would it be possible to find the contractor involved?"

Carla leaned back in the chair. "Happydoo will need to locate the appointment files—I'm not confident that personnel details would have been included. One expects a company covering contracts of this nature to employ the very best there is."

Happydoo's camera-eyes lit up a brilliant blue. *'I am accessing the very files you were speaking of, Master Beckett. Give me a minute while I find the contractor's employment records.'*

A few beads of perspiration broke out on my brow as I waited patiently for him to select the file. Carla reached out a hand to pat the android affectionately on the back. "You are such a superstar, Happydoo."

Happydoo reacted in predictable fashion. *'I am happy to do it Mrs. Carla.'*

A few seconds later he found the relevant section. *'The contractor assigned to install the sign-in software was, Sign-secure Systems Ltd. They are based in Quantum City's Industrial dis-*

trict and appear to be a large international con-
tractor, doing all New World Earth Military
software installations for quantum-based sign-in
applications.'

The military establishment and its appointment of lieutenant Sparkle grew with sudden
exponential interest. My gut-feel ascribed intent
and piled it up against the military's door. Any
contractor involved with a potential war-monger,
would be susceptible to bribes and favors in the
hope of a lucrative contract. It would be easy for
one of the generals or senior administrators to
dangle a fat contract for a small change to the protocols. I voiced my opinion to Carla and Happydoo.

Carla did not share all my enthusiasm. "You
may be jumping to a conclusion, Hon—the military
higher-ups can be corrupt but we still lack a motive. I know several of the generals who were involved with Dr. Abrams—they are good soldiers
with impeccable records and I can't see any of
them risking their reputations on something like
this."

She made a good point but my hypothesis
still warranted consideration.

Happydoo interrupted our back and forth.
'Sign-Secure Systems did supply the names of
their top personnel to be involved with the system.
These are:

Project Manager: T. Bronson; Shift Supervisors: D. Emanuel and C. Pearson; Installation: H. Dubrowski and S. Watkins. The installation of the software and testing took only three days, Master Beckett.'

At first I didn't make the connection with one of the names but Carla did.

"Did you say, Pearson?"

'Yes Mrs. Carla—C. Pearson.'

She turned to stare at me and I read her thoughts. Our XO, Gary Pearson's, younger brother went by the name of Colin.

∞∞

Eighteen

Excerpt from the President Commander's Log.

January, 2345 CE.
......it is hard to believe that twenty-one years have come and gone since we left Earth's solar system. There is a growing attitude of expectation as the Andromeda hurtles at mind-blowing speed through space—the completion of each hibernation period serving as a welcomed milestone for our epic journey......group A has the Con.

Carla and I processed through the standard resuscitation procedure after the 7th hibernation period with the usual queasiness which lasted for about a week. It became customary for me to spend the first two days, with the President Commander's log in the presence of Gary Pearson, a tiresome but important practice. I needed to know details of important events on my XO's watch. At the completion of my task he would enter hibernation with group B.

The overall economics painted its own picture of reality—a balance of provision with consumption proved a challenge. Did all business in the area we called "Andromeda City," meet expectations? How the staff handled hazardous emergencies?

Earlier discussions with Ozzy, about the attempt to eliminate Carla and I from leadership, rendered a decision to maintain a constant vigilance. The alien believed the perpetrator would overplay his hand at some future point in time. Whoever planned the extreme measure also, by this time, knew of its failure. There remained ample opportunity for another attempt. Mickey continued to monitor all the protocols of each hibernation process and, as a security measure, the main-frame chamber placed in lock-down to all but Carla and I.

In casual conversation with Gary Pearson we established the position with regard to his younger brother, Colin. The two had not spoken for many years, due to a fall out over a land inheritance. The information gleaned from Happydoo and Carla's research thus remained unconcluded.

As time passed Carla and I spent many a moment at the forward visual ports. We flew through many star systems, the closest star 1.5 light years distant from the Andromeda, provided a wonderful sight which we gawped at for hours. At times I asked Mickey to provide a telescopic view on the holo-platform, to give us front-row seats of gas giants and spectacular nebulas. We often consulted the astrogator 3-d maps and try to put names to them but after a while the practice became tiresome. It did help us though, to appreciate the enormity of space—to perceive the great expanse between stars and how futile our journey would have been without a high-percentage light-speed capability.

A month into group B's seventh hibernation period, Ozzy paid us a welcomed visit. He greeted me with his usual sense of humor.

"Greetings Earthling, how was your induced sleep?"

"Just fine my good friend. I see you visited the Andromeda quite frequently while I was regurgitating the green fluid."

"Yes—that's true. Please don't take umbrage at the fact I do not always visit you as frequently. It's just I felt your XO needed me around more often. I managed to talk him out of some dubious decisions."

"I read about some of them in the log—I must extend my thanks to you. Gary is not very good with people and he tends to be a bit autocratic when dealing with staff-related problems," I said.

Ozzy made the weird compressed-air sound, which I did not have an interpretation for—my best guess, he agreed to disagree. We talked about several of the emergency situations Gary dealt with and the advice the alien gave until he changed the subject.

"I have some important news about the Crustans. It comes from one of our advanced scout organizations working just inside the Lumbrian dimension, close to the portal that serves the general area of your intended destination. Not only do they appear to have established a small recon group on the planet you seek, they have also extended their activity to several smaller planets in the region."

A chill shot through my system—not the news I wanted hear. "How close have they ventured in our general direction?"

"The last report stated their radius of activity to be approximately three or four light-years from Hera-Soter. The task force doing their pioneering is not very big but certainly a formidable one. It's possible they are looking for certain minerals to mine."

"So...we'll run into them sometime during the last seven year period of our journey?"

"I'm afraid so—the size of the colony on Hera-Soter is relatively small at this time, however, that could change."

My mind assessed the ramifications of the alien's response. "Perhaps it's time to discuss what we are likely to experience if our paths cross with these war-mongers."

Ozzy wheezed, blew out air and bobbed all at once. The single, large eye blinked in a rapid sequence, while he composed himself to further discuss the matter.

"You will recall my description of the Crustan anatomy—they are bipedal with four arms and claw-like pincers that are very flexible. They do not have skin as you do but their entire bodies are encased with a type of a crustacean shell of a bright blue color. These blue ones are the military drones whose minds are all linked on a single wavelength with a leader. The leaders are bright red in color and have some autonomy of thought but are largely controlled by the supreme Crustan leader who is their king."

I remembered Ozzy's description of the enemy from some of our previous conversations and imagined the lack of Crustan autonomy to be an advantage to us. But it worked two ways—the disadvantage might be their expendability to their king.

Ozzy wheezed and continued. "While in space the Crustans wear a protective suit over their shell exteriors and a system that keeps life-supporting fluid circulating. These suits maintain the fluid at a constant temperature, much like your own. We will discuss their weaknesses and it will be your responsibility to work out ways of exploiting them."

*

While Ozzy and I discussed the expected future confrontation with the Crustans Carla spent time with Happydoo, in examination of the many issues recorded by the android while we endured our most recent hibernation. It appeared our XO, Gary Pearson and a certain member of staff, met together on a regular basis. They also formed a strong alliance at all executive meetings.

I did not have a problem with close relationships between crew members. In the case of singles it often became preferable for people to find partners of their choice on long voyages and when Carla mentioned this particular relationship I did not think too much on it. She, however, saw it from a different perspective.

∞∞

Nineteen

First Contact

Excerpt from the President Commander's Log:

January, 2365 CE.

.....our periods of hibernation are officially over. The XO and his group will once again enjoy time together with us, to face the final seven years of space travel as a complete crew. Unfortunately the menace of which Ozzy had warned us was about to rear its ugly head—the Crustans are waiting....

Carla gazed wistfully out at the black expanse of space. "How far are we from Hera-Soter, Hon?"

I asked Mickey to do a quick calculation and the answer came straight back without hesitation. *'We are 4.23 lightyears from the planet—still another seven years of travel, President Commander.'*

I somberly reminisced on the disturbing facts about the status of our home planet. "I still can't believe the Earth is going to become a barren waste—the entire solar system, for that fact."

Carla flinched and glanced at the Earth Dynamical Clock behind the Con. It showed thirty-eight years lapsed on Earth, to twenty-one years endured for our journey. "At least they have plenty of time before the neutron star enters the solar system—it's fantastic to think, that millions of our people will start the same epic journey, before the end comes."

"Let's hope we'll have established a descent home for them by the time they arrive on Hera-Soter. The later craft will be more sophisticated than the Andromeda so the more recent travelers might be able to make the journey quicker," I said.

"Relativity is such a strange concept. At least we know it actually works—we are the living proof. You hardly look a day older than you did when we left, Hon."

I laughed. "Thanks to Einstein we can work out what happens at near light speed. The hibernation process also has something to do with our lack of aging. You're as beautiful as the day I met you, sweetheart."

Carla loved it when I paid her compliments.

"We can't even begin to think of establishing anything until the Crustan threat is dealt with."

I grunted. "Ozzy and I have been discussing the issue at length. We're devising a way to strengthen our protective energy-shields and a new design of canon is being looked over by our engineering division as we speak. It works on the basis of firing anti-matter particles which destroy targeted matter progressively."

"Sounds dangerous but effective—don't bother trying to explain the science behind it. I wouldn't understand."

I gave her a mischievous look. "Don't worry, I wouldn't even try—don't understand it myself, Babe."

Our verbal reverie came to an abrupt end with the appearance of Happydoo.

'Could I speak with you and Mrs. Carla in private, Master Beckett?'

The on-duty ensign appeared to be busy with some reports and I wondered what prompted the android's request for privacy. The main console is at least thirty feet from the forward view ports—the possibility of the ensign's ability to eavesdrop on our conversation seemed unlikely.

I raised my eyebrows. "What's up, Happydoo?"

'Please follow me, Master Beckett.' He turned and walked off the bridge.

The stern look on Happydoo's face signified the need not to question but to follow. In all the years of service to my family I never knew him to act this way before. Android valets are programmed to be compliant, not to ever issue instructions to a human being unless their status demanded it. With a sideways glance at the ensign Carla and I left the general bridge area in the android's wake. We took the verticap to the cargo area, where Happydoo led us to a location, adjacent to the Orbitron. The android turned to address us.

'Forgive my clandestine behavior, Master Beckett but this is one of the very few safe areas for our discussion.'

"Safe area? What are you talking about, Happydoo?"

'It would seem the places you and Mrs. Carla frequent on a daily basis have all been bugged with a very special listening device.'

Carla's eyes opened wide in shock. "We are being spied on?"

'Yes, Mrs. Carla—someone has placed these small devices in many of the spots where you and Master Beckett have conversations. I discovered the first one quite by accident. Then I started looking for more and found them all over the place.'

My mind dredged out all the suspicions with regards to the mystery person, or persons, who wanted us eliminated. The strong alliance formed between our XO, Gary, and Laura Samuels now took center stage. A thought struck me—could the two of them have formed a conspiracy to take over leadership of the project?

"All these other devices are obviously still in place—you haven't removed any?"

The android shook his head. *'I thought it better to allow whoever is trying to listen in a measure of complacency. That way we can feed false information and induce the perpetrator to take some action which might lead to exposure.'*

I experienced a rush of affection for my valet. He took responsibility to save my bacon at every necessary occasion. "Happydoo, words cannot convey how thankful I am for you."

The android reacted in typical fashion with the pirouette, foot-stomp routine, accompanied by the stretch of synthetic skin around its mouth, to form a huge Cheshire grin. The eyes shone with a brilliant blue light that pulsed and mimicked the action of an ancient slot-machine. Although it's a feature of a program I could not help appreciate the aspect of joy Happydoo would show when a compliment came his way.

'I am happy to do anything for you and Mrs. Carla, Master Beckett.'

Carla gave a short laugh but then became serious. "We'll have to bait the hook for our listener and see if anything comes of it. Can you give us a list of the safe spots, Happydoo?"

*

Later, Carla and I retired to bed for the night with much to think about and at 0130 hours my mind, still in a state of turmoil, resisted sleep. Carla appeared to have won the battle. I listened to the cadence of her breath as she slept beside me and I reached out a hand to touch the locks of the beautiful, long hair as it flowed over her shoulders. I would be devastated if I ever lost her.

An emergency light on the control panel at the door awakened me from my reflections. Mickey's smooth, calm voice broke the silence.

'President Commander? I detect through the bio-rhythm monitor you are still awake.'

"What is it, Mickey? It's unlike you to strike up a conversation after I've hit the sack—are you lonely?"

'I am never lonely, President Commander. I thought you should know my forward sensors have picked up a heat signature ahead of us. It is definitely a craft of some sort but the distance is still too great to tell what sort of propulsion system is being used. I have alerted Lieutenant Commander Pearson.'

"I will be on the bridge in a minute or two—thanks, Mickey."

'You are welcome, boss.'

Gary Pearson and I arrived on the bridge at the same time. I did not wake Carla as the effects of the recent hibernation still lingered in both our systems and the more natural sleep we could get the better for full recovery.

A concerned frown straddled the brow of the ensign who sat in the commander's seat at the Con. He leapt to his feet and vacated the seat for me as Gary and I approached.

"What are you seeing out there ensign?" I asked.

"It's definitely a craft under power, President Commander. Our present trajectory will bring us within a stone's throw of each other in about twenty minutes—they are approaching at a speed of one-half C."

Gary leaned forward to peer at the interferometer screen. "What's their trajectory in relation to ours?"

The ensign tapped a key on the con-panel and the screen produced a graphic 2-d picture of the two ship's trajectories. A further tap on the key and the holo-receiver platform came to life with a 3-d representation. It showed the foreign craft on an approach at a steep trajectory, from a lower elevation.

The ensign switched to another screen and a picture of the unknown craft appeared in the shape of a fuzzy round ball of green light with a visible propulsion plume of energy behind it. We all stood transfixed to the spot, our eyes glued to the screen as the fuzziness took a more definite shape. I needed to determine if this craft belonged to a Crustan scout party.

"Mickey—call Ozzy to the bridge."

'Certainly, President Commander.'

We did not take our eyes off the image and within a few minutes a cylindrical vessel, with fins like a shark, materialized. The distance between the two craft diminished. My mind became mesmerized by the image until a tap on my shoulder shocked me out of the fixation. Ozzy floated close behind me, to peer over my shoulder at the screen. The alien stared at the image for a long while.

"It's a Crustan prospecting vessel. You can be sure they have already spotted us and will have called back to their most forward base. This vessel is not armed but in a short space of time we can expect a Crustan Destroyer."

∞∞

Twenty

An Unwelcome Visitor

Returning to our quarters I found Carla still fast asleep and for a moment all the tension, regarding the discovery of the Crustan prospecting vessel, evaporated. She looked so serene with her curvaceous form revealed in its fullness, beneath the scanty sleeping garment. The sight created an instant desire within me—I wanted to run my hands over the curves, to cradle her head and kiss her lips. I resisted the strong impulse to awaken her and make copious love. My selfish thoughts dissolved in an instant—she needed the sleep. With gentleness I lay beside her and buried my face into the back of her neck. Sleep for me, however, would not come—all the latest discoveries, danced across the stage of my imagination.

In the morning, while eating breakfast, I sprung the news of the Crustan vessel's appearance.

"I wondered how long it would be before we ran into them," she said.

"The sooner we get to know exactly what we're up against the better we can plan things. Ozzy is convinced the prospecting vessel will contact one of their warships which he thinks could be holed up at a forward base, somewhere in the constellation."

"How are we progressing with the strengthening of Andromeda's protective shields and the new weaponry system?"

"The shields now have an extra barrier in the form of a magnetic bubble between the inner and outer energy fields, giving the ship's hull a much greater resistance to enemy ordinance."

"And the anti-thingamajig you spoke of?"

"I assume you're referring to the anti-matter attack canon Ozzy introduced for our arsenal?"

Carla closed her eyes and smiled. "Whatever, sweetheart—you know exactly what I'm talking about."

"We have to convert our small on-board particle accelerator to produce the anti-matter needed and then come up with a containment casing. The engineering staff is working on the details but the finished product will take some time."

"What happens if the Crustan warship arrives before its ready?"

"We'll have to deal with it—our nukes will be pretty efficient in providing a credible deterrent. I doubt the Crustans will want to risk an immediate confrontation with an alien ship until they have investigated."

She remained thoughtful while I went into the ablution chamber. Half-an hour later we approached the bridge to find Gary Pearson engaged in a conversation with Laura Samuels. Carla and I agreed not to let on about our suspicions. We made every effort to be as congenial as possible.

The on-duty ensign watched over the con while Gary and Laura chatted. They stood close to each other and stared out of the forward viewing port as Carla and I approached the con. The ensign stood to greet us. Out of the corner of my eye I noticed Laura peel away from Gary and make for the bridge stairs. In passing us by, she ignored me and flashed a brief smile at Carla. Over the years I tried several times to engage her in conversation, but the issue of my complicity in her husband's death during the reactor fire debacle, still stood like a barrier in our way. I also tried to avoid her a lot of the time, in the belief she would never forgive me—a possible fact I would have to live with.

Carla and I decided, on this particular day, to leave a snippet of information for whoever listened in on our conversations. This piece of intelligence would make them think a significant discovery on our behalf would soon lead us to the perpetrator. No names, other than the details of the company involved in the installation of the sign-in program, would be mentioned plus our excitement of a significant breakthrough made on an identity.

The deed might not cause any immediate hostile reaction but we could at least pay extra attention to any changes in attitude, be it Gary Pearson, Laura Samuels or whoever. Happydoo continued to check on the positions of the listening devices. He also tried to find out where the master receiver might be situated. Mickey, could monitor all signals tied into the ship's communication, but could not pin-point the position of a clandestine system. My intuition told me the perpetrator would act, in some way to gain control, during this final period of travel. Everyone knew about the Crustan threat—even all the folk going about their normal business in Andromeda City. We would soon have more than an unsubstantiated, internal threat on our hands, to worry about.

Gary appeared to be in a good mood as he moved toward the con. A pleasant smile adorned his face and he seemed at ease. Carla and I continued to view a record of the Crustan prospecting vessel's sudden retreat, which must have happened on detection of the Andromeda's presence.

"Morning, Beckett—Carla," he chirped.

We acknowledged his greeting and turned back to the screen. "I see our visitor beat a hasty retreat." I said.

The XO laughed. "I think they got a terrible fright. The Andromeda is probably nothing like they've ever encountered before—just our sheer size must have scared the living shit out of them."

"I doubt whether one of their bigger brothers would have the same reaction. Ozzy maintains some of the Crustan warships are pretty huge."

"Do we have any clue as to how long it will be before one comes along," asked Carla.

"None at all. We'll just have to wait and be ready," I said. "We may be able to deal with one but I'm hoping that two or three don't show up together."

I heard a wheeze behind me and turned my head to see Ozzy floating toward the Con. His humor, as always, raised the ambiance on the bridge.

"Greetings Earthlings—how are you, Carla, my dear?" His soft spot for her showed. He would stretch out two of his stubby arms, to touch each of her shoulders with the short, three-fingered hands, bob, wheeze and suck in air—no one else got this special treatment in a greeting. I assumed it to be the equivalent of a human hug.

"I have a question for you, my alien friend," I said. "How fast is the Crustan communication through space? What method do they use to send their messages to one another?"

The large eye oscillated a few times. "They have a system that uses quantum entangled particles—similar to the method your scientists have been looking at for ages but haven't as yet resolved."

"Do the Lumbrians also use this method?"

"No, dear friend, no. The Lumbrians use a means that can only be understood in our dimension. My Orbitron maintains connection to our dimension so I am able to keep in contact with my peers while here with you. We have never needed to use quantum entanglement but the Crustans have a similar universe to yours in terms of matter, so they have forged ahead with QE."

I experienced a nervous shudder. "You are saying they will have instantaneous communications?"

"Oh yes, definitely."

"So....the Crustan warship will probably be here sooner than we expected?"

"The sooner the better, my friend. We will see what their reaction to our presence will be in a very short space of time."

As if to frame Ozzy's answers Mickey made a sudden announcement.

'Foreign craft approaching on our port side, President Commander.'

A panic rose within me. "How far away, Mickey?"

'It is still forty Light-minutes out and not distinguishable as yet.'

"Give us an immediate visual when it reaches twenty light-minutes, please."

'Will do, President Commander.'

Carla spoke first, after we all sustained a short but palpable silence. "What are we going to do, Beckett?"

From behind us, a smooth, digitized voice filled the atmosphere. *'May I suggest we adhere to the NWE Military rules of engagement, President Commander.'*

Taken by surprise I swung around, thinking it to be my valet, but the intense blue eyes of Lieutenant Sparkle stared back at me.

"Sparkle, you startled me—I didn't hear you step onto the bridge."

'My apologies, President Commander. I did not mean to intrude but my processor picked up the messages regarding Mickey's observation of the alien craft.'

I experienced a bit prickliness about the incursion made by the android but remembered the mandate given it by Dr. Abrams. We consulted with Sparkle on many issues which affected the folk in Andromeda City, over the duration of the voyage and I met regularly with a delegation of the original dissenters whenever something arose, which might have an effect on the mission as a whole. Since the incident of the Solar Star, our consultations remained at a minimum but this time Sparkle's military persuasion might serve us well, given an imminent confrontation with the Crustans.

"Familiarize me with those rules, Lieutenant."

∞∞

Twenty-one

Crustan Warships

'The craft can now be clearly seen, President Commander.'

The 3-d image of the Crustan warship appeared on the holo-receiver. It looked intimidating and formidable. Three protrusions extended from the front and spiraled to pin-sharp points, like spears—to ram the prey, if all else failed. The hull, made of a black, metallic material sported short, scythe-shaped wings and the absence of internal or external illumination meant they ran dark. On each side of the hull, short, stubby protrusions could be seen and I took these to be weapons. On further, careful examination the weapons appeared on the underside as well as on the top. It bristled with armaments.

"What do you think, Ozzy?"

The alien wheezed and bobbed. "It's a typical Crustan warship—of the destroyer class. Lumbrian Intelligence reports they saw three of these monsters cross into your universe. I'm not sure if we'll see a second ship, following in this one's wake. It depends on how great they deem the threat to be."

In my discussion with Lieutenant Sparkle the first rule of engagement seemed a sensible one, although given the Crustan mindset, this might be debatable: *not to engage if a war has not been declared.* The second rule provided me with more confidence: *If fired upon by an enemy, obvious evasive action needed to be taken—return fire to be initiated, the type of weapon to be decided by Mickey's incoming ordinance, analysis detectors.* The defense system, designed to operate under the guidance of the Master AI computer could be overridden by the human Commander of the ship, if he decided it to be in the best interests of the engagement.

The lieutenant made it clear he would stand by in an advisory capacity and not interfere with any of the decisions I made. All personal in Andromeda City, the secular working folk, made their way to the escape pods and the flight staff remained at their posts for further notice. This would be the first real test of our resilience and my leadership acumen in a confrontational situation. We would also find out how vulnerable the Andromeda might be in the face of Crustan military capability. Our newest weapon, the anti-matter canon, existed in theory—a prototype still under construction.

"In your experience, regarding these confrontations, do you think they will attack us without hesitation, Ozzy?"

"I don't think so but we need to be ready. This is really a first contact which is different to the Crustan, Lumbrian situation, where we have been at war for years. I personally think they will observe us for a short period—maybe even try to communicate with us."

I regained a measure of composure. "That would make sense. Do you understand their language?"

"To a degree, however, it can be difficult because they speak very quickly—in short bursts of clucks and clicks—I have a language translator in the Orbitron which we will make use of."

Gary Pearson interrupted. "Will they not suspect a Lumbrian might be aboard with the use of your technology?"

Ozzy hesitated before speaking. "They might, but if you're unable to answer them back they may fire upon us. We will just have to lead them to believe you have the technology."

Mickey's voice permeated the bridge. 'Foreign vessel is now ten light-minutes away and altering course, President Commander.'

I looked at the graphic trajectory screen and watched the warship cut a slow arc toward our position, posturing to cut across our stern. I guessed the commander's tactic would be to follow us from a safe distance, off our starboard bow. "What speed are they doing, Mickey?"

'Their approach before de-acceleration, matched our present speed of 75 percent C, President Commander. The warship will have to exceed this figure to catch us after execution of the maneuver.'

I inclined my head to give Ozzy a questioning glance.

"The Crustan vessels have been known to get within 90 percent C in their own dimension which is, as I have mentioned previously, very similar to your own universe."

Carla raised her eyebrows. "I guess we won't be able to outrun them, then."

A silence followed as we all contemplated the odds. Mickey's voice, again, filled the confines of the bridge area. *'Foreign warship has executed turn and is rapidly approaching our starboard bow, President Commander.'*

We could all see this on the graphic trajectory screen. The speed with which the vessel caught us astounded me and my mind screamed for a solution. I noticed Ozzy wore a flat plate-like pad on one of his arms, above one of the stubby three-fingered hands. I assumed he came prepared with a device, which gave access to the Orbitron's array of equipment.

Our eyes remained glued to the trajectory screen. The Crustan vessel crept alongside us, to match our momentum and stayed there. I wondered what thoughts might be passing through the Crustan Commander's mind.

A light blinked on the console. Mickey responded with his usual coolness.

'There is a communication from the warship, President Commander—it is on the frequency set for emergency contacts.'

Ozzy removed the plate-like pad from his arm and passed it to me. "When the Crustan speaks you need to press the red key. For your answer, release the red key and use the green one— the translator's operation is simple. I have set it for Crustan-human language."

I took the translator in my hand with a quiver of apprehension. "Is the incoming signal compatible with our holo-receiver, Mickey?" I moved over to the receiving platform. If the signal provided some compatibility to our system I might be able to see the Crustan speaker and he should be able to see me. We all prepared ourselves for the first visage of the enemy. We did not have long to wait.

The holo-receiver crackled to life as a hologram of the Crustan formed on the platform. There appeared to be enough compatibility between the two systems.

My first glimpse of the alien remains etched into my memory. The fierce countenance, and thick crab-like appendages, folded across a large shell-plated torso, drew gasps from all of us except

Ozzy. The creature's head looked more like a football, with large scales above each of its two eyes. The scale resembled an eye-brow and eye-lid, rolled into one. The snout, ended with a small gap which served as a mouth and showed sharp, jagged teeth.   The Crustans did not appear to wear clothes, accept for a cape draped around the protrusions, which seemed to serve as shoulders for the appendages. The robe, a bright green color, obscured the view of the alien's lower half.

We all stared dumbfounded at the grotesqueness of our enemy and a series of clicks and clucks emanated from the hologram as it addressed us. I jammed my finger on the translator's red button to catch the translation.

".....yourself. I will give you three photo-periods. If you do not comply we will extinguish your breath."

Glancing across at Ozzy's impassive features I understood the translator's ability to convert Crustan words to English still needed some tweaking. "I guess it's asking us to identify ourselves or get blown out of the universe."

Ozzy bobbed and farted air. "Something like that."

I pressed the green key and hoped my words would be clear and concise. "We are a pioneering group from a distant solar system. My name is Beckett Conroy. I am a human and the commander of this vessel."

Silence reigned for a minute while the alien considered my words. I hoped his translator would do its job.

"Why have you violated sovereign Crustan space, Human, Beckett Conroy?"

The commander's deception, to make us think they inhabited the Pegasus area, became clear.

I subdued the inclination to call him on the ruse and maintained a calm demeanor. "Our quest is to find a new habitat for our kind. Our solar system has been invaded by a neutron star and rendered uninhabitable. Our space technology has not shown there to be any occupants in this region. To whom am I speaking?"

Another delay—I forgot to depress the red key for the return communication but we didn't miss anything. The foreign commander seemed to be contemplating my words.

"I am Torban, the chief overseer of this destroyer. We are the Crustans and are occupying this part of space for the purpose of mining minerals." The translation appeared to evolve in clarity and improved grammar with each communication.

"We come in peace, Chief Overseer, Torban. Although we do carry arms our craft is chiefly an exploration vessel."

Again, a short silence ensued before Torban spoke. On hearing his words my blood ran cold.

∞∞

Twenty-two

Alien Confrontation

"Listen to me carefully human, Beckett Conroy. You are in violation of this space. You will point out where the entrance to your vessel is. We are going to extend a boarding tube and enter your craft. You will receive our soldiers meekly and without resistance—consider yourselves our prisoners. If you refuse this we will have no option but to dispose of you and your ship."

I sensed a panic rise within the small group, gathered around the Con. We stared at each other with open mouths, lost for words. Lieutenant Sparkle jarred our mental inertia.

'We cannot allow them to board our ship, President Commander.'

My thoughts came back on track with a sudden rush of adrenaline. Prodding the green key on the translator to open my line of communication, I addressed the alien commander.

"Listen carefully, Chief Overseer, Torban. While I admire your call to duty I question the veracity of your decision. We are a peaceful group of pioneers who do not seek to be at war with you and your species. If you pursue a peaceful relationship with us we will reciprocate—however, should you choose conflict, we as humans will respond accordingly."

A short silence ensued before the hologram materialized again. Torban's eyes seemed to open wider and the cruel mouth revealed the jagged line of teeth in what could be interpreted as a sneer.

"You have no idea of our military prowess, human. We are the supreme rulers of all space—now, in the name of our king, Loreth the great, point out where your entrance is—we are coming aboard."

"You are making a great error in judgement, Chief Overseer. I doubt whether your king will commend you for bringing destruction to your own warship. You will not board our vessel."

I turned to the others and raised my hand in a gesture, seeking their agreement. The solemn looks all round reflected the general sentiment but no one questioned my response.

Ozzy wheezed and spluttered, his huge round eye blinked with rapid succession. "You need to take evasive action immediately and consider yourselves to be at war with the Crustans. I do not know the full extent of the Andromeda's military capabilities but I have full confidence in your capacity to meet the current danger. Please do not think I am deserting you—unfortunately I cannot risk any damage to the Orbitron so I will need to leave for a period of time."

We all understood Ozzy's dilemma and I sought to reassure him. "We really appreciate your support for our mission and will earnestly await your return when circumstances allow it. You have been our greatest source of encouragement over the years."

We all said a quick goodbye to our alien friend and he departed to the verticap with a wave of farewell as the capsule swallowed him for quick transfer to the cargo hold.

Mickey spelled out a sudden warning. *'Please strap yourselves into the gravity couches. Lieutenant Sparkle and I have linked processors and full use of his Diamond 1000 military prowess is now at our disposal.'*

During the latter part of my discussion with the Crustan commander, Sparkle moved over to the vertical instrument array behind the con and settled into an android communication station. With four fingers of the right hand, locked into a processor-linking module, the deep blue lights behind his camera eyes pulsated at a rapid rate.

Mickey calmly shared the status quo. *'Crustan warship has broken away and is moving rapidly to obtain a safe firing range. Orbitron is clear of the Andromeda and melting into the Lumbrian dimension.'*

For the moment, my input would not be required. The two AI's would process all the necessary telemetry and initiate engagement protocol. I wondered what Mickey would have done without the Diamond 1000.

'Enemy warship now at one light-minute. Andromeda shield protection is at full strength.'

The holographic receiver flared to life, bringing us a visual of the two ships. The warship turned to present us with its back-end and all the protrusions aft turned in our direction.

'Firing range for Andromeda's tactical nuke missiles is now at optimum. Permission to fire, President Commander.'

The moment threatened to overwhelm me. Adrenaline pumped viciously into my system as I fought to keep a level head. It would be a violation of the first rule of engagement if we fired first—it may also be a squandering of our last opportunity if I allowed them to fire before we did. I looked toward Sparkle, his two blue eyes locked onto mine—he nodded his head.

"Fire, Mickey. There is no time like the present."

The timing may have seemed coincidental because the enemy fired at the same instant. We saw the release of pressure from two of the stubby, missile muzzles, each firing its package of destruction at us. The Andromeda, being a much larger vessel, presented the easier target but I knew our heat-seekers would lock on to the warship's propulsion plume. Much of their deliverance, as ours, would depend on the strength of the ships protective shield and the effectiveness of its evasive abilities.

'There are missiles incoming—prepare for countermeasure maneuvers—intercept flares deployed.'

Our fate would rest in the efficacy of the Andromeda's protective technology and the strength of the enemy's ordinance. I hoped the former would prove a life-saving grace and the latter to be the enemy's greatest failure. We would know in a short space of time. The entire scenario played out on the holographic receiver which made it easy for us to time our actions in response to the Crustan threat. The intercept flares diverted one of the missiles and it missed the Andromeda. The second missile, however, did not veer off its course.

'Prepare for imminent missile impact—angle of ship's shield adjusting to provide maximum hull protection.'

Time seemed to turn into eternity as we all prepared ourselves for the enemy missile to explode against the ship's protective shield. There would be ramifications. Even if the Andromeda survived the initial shock-wave, a breached hull remained a strong possibility, and radiation from the blast would contaminate the impacted area.

Ozzy's intervention during the course of the mission provided a huge saving grace for the Andromeda—the upgrading of the ship's protective shields. The missile's total destructive force would depend on the angle our new shield technology could manage, thus producing a glancing-off effect as opposed to a direct hit.

The explosion, when it came, shook the entire vessel with tremendous force and for a moment it seemed we would break into a thousand pieces. The normal tranquil peace of the bridge shattered into a myriad of alarms; red lights glowed and pulsated and several claxons, screamed like banshees. Carla, strapped to the couch next to me, shrieked and reached over to grab my hand, with a vice-like grip. Gary croaked out a gasp of fear and I shut my eyes as the Andromeda turned over onto its side and appeared to wobble for a few brief seconds.

"Talk to me, Mickey," I shouted.

The Andromeda righted itself again and hope of our survival flourished. For an instant it appeared the vessel might roll over in a prolonged death spiral.

'Checking all systems, President Commander. I will have a full damage report as soon as it is complete.'

"Has the hull been breached?—are we still in one piece?"

'The Hull has been breached, President Commander, but only minimally. I have sealed off sectors H-303 and 304. The internal hull-resealing bots are locked in and performing their tasks. We are still in one piece.'

Pressure from our restraints indicated the loss of the ship's normal gravity load. If I tried to release the r-bar's, zero G would cause me to fly out of the seat. This did not trouble me but the thought of floating around in darkness provided enough deterrent to stay put for the time-being.

The emergency lighting circuit might have been damaged as it should have come on immediately. As if reading my thoughts, Mickey made another announcement.

'Emergency lighting damaged—circuit under repair by techno-bots and will activate shortly. Please remain in your seats.'

Interminable moments passed as we waited for the emergency lighting. Apart from the dull red and orange pulsating of alarm icons the darkness threatened to smother us. I could hear Carla's soft sob next to me, her hand still with a tight grip on my forearm. Then it occurred to me—what about the enemy?

"Are the heat-signature sensors still working, Mickey? Is there any sign of the enemy warship?"

'Heat-signature sensors are ineffective due to the immense amount of radiation generated by

the strike, President Commander. We will pass through the strike-zone cloud in a minute, or so. The holo-cameras are not able to see anything at this time.'

Each passing moment now became a reason for celebration. The perspiration floated off my face as we waited for another explosion to end our cosmic existence. Carla appeared to have regained her composure while Gary and the on-duty ensign remained quiet. We all contemplated the predicament in terms of the lack of information at our disposal—the Andromeda's future looked bleak.

After what seemed an eternity of waiting, but in real time took about thirty seconds, Mickey's calm and resolute voice broke through the cacophony of alarms.

'Enemy warship is dead ahead, President Commander.'

∞∞

Twenty-three

Surviving the Onslaught

'There appears to be no propulsion plume and the craft's impetus has fallen off to .5 C, President Commander.'

"Can you ping it to see if the protective shields are activated?"

'No shield is in place, Boss. The vessel seems to be without power. I detect significant damage to the rear. They must have received a direct hit from one of our heat-seekers.'

The emergency lights came on with a dull glimmer to bathe the bridge in an incandescent glow. We took stock of the immediate surroundings and breathed huge sighs of relief. Apart from the alarms that did not cancel automatically, all seemed to be in order. I released the couch restraint bar and floated out of the couch, to grab Carla's out-stretched hand.

"Are you able to restore gravity, Mickey?"

'There are techno-bots working on it as we speak, Boss. I estimate ten more minutes.'

"The escape pods—is everything still intact?"

'The City folk are all shaken but not any the worse for wear. All flight personnel managed to strap in before the strike and there are no casualties, President Commander.'

"Fantastic—you okay, Carla?—Gary?"

They both affirmed their well-being. Gary had a huge grin on his face.

"That fucking alien crab—king of all fucking space, is he? They got what was coming to them."

"We don't know what their status is, so let's not count our chickens before they hatch—we need to be wary."

Carla pulled herself toward me, folded her arms around my waist and burrowed her cheek into my neck.

"I thought we were dead for sure. I love you, sweetheart."

I could feel her whole body shaking from the shock of it all.

"Luv you too, Hon."

A holographic image sprung to life on the receiver and we could see the enemy warship. It hung in the space ahead of us, benignly lifeless and the longer I stared the more my intuition gnawed away at rational thought.

The on-duty ensign cancelled the active alarms and the icons changed to a constant red glow. The ensuing silence added to the eerie effect of the emergency lights. I looked across at Lieutenant Sparkle. He remained in his seat, fingers of the right hand still locked into the input port, which connected his processor to Mickey's system—he would remain there until the threat de-escalated.

"Keep the city people in their pods, Mickey. Let them know danger still lurks and we're checking it out. Slow the Andromeda to match the warship's velocity."

*

The executive flight crew gathered themselves together in the boardroom where Carla, Gary and I prepared to brief them. With the restoration of the ship's internal gravity and lights, life returned to normal. The remainder of the Con's red alarm icons referred to sectors, H-303 and 304, now sealed off due to breaches in the hull. The repair bots, inside the sectors worked to apply a liquid graphene metal to the ruptured hull. The prognosis remained positive—we would have the use of these sections once the radiation returned to safe levels.

Lieutenant Sparkle decided to move himself from the bridge to a wall-charging station at the back of the room, where he could still maintain a link with Mickey.

I supplied all the facts to the flight supervisors in charge of navigation, propulsion, maintenance and life support stability.

"We have survived a nuclear missile strike launched by a Crustan warship. As I have shared with you before, the Crustans are only intent on one thing—to annihilate anyone they see as opposition. We had no option but to refuse their demand to board our ship and the Crustan leader consider us his prisoners."

One of the number raised a hand to ask a question. "Are we still vulnerable, President Commander?"

"We are hoping the threat has passed, however, our alien friend, Ozzy, did mention their scouts detected three of these warships slipping into our universe from the Crustan dimension."

Another supervisor, a tall man with a beard, slipped up his hand. "I understand the warship that attacked us is disabled—what will we do to make sure it's not a trap?"

"That is a very good question and the answer is one which we must decide on right away—time is of the essence. If the craft is playing possum and waiting for us to get closer then we need to destroy it completely. Should it be totally disabled then we need to know what the crew is doing."

The bearded supervisor raised his hand again. "Are you thinking of boarding the vessel? I think the safest route is to destroy them immediately."

A senior propulsion manager, a buxom woman in her forties, stood to counter the man's argument.

"We can't just destroy them without checking on what their status is. If their shields are not in operation it means they have no means of securing their vessel. Who would take such a chance—to not protect themselves, if it were possible?"

Gary waded into the fray. "It could be a trap. They may be gambling on the fact we are a peaceful species—we told them as much."

Everyone wanted to voice an opinion at the same time so I brought the meeting to order. Sparkle, however, preempted my attempt.

'I have a suggestion for the President Commander to consider.'

From the back of the room, the sound of his digital purr, elevated above the general cacophony of voices, caused everyone to turn and stare.

'It may be a trap, or the Crustan crew might be dead. There is still another possibility— the crew may have evacuated via escape pods. Mickey's sensors show a significant explosive event on the warship at about the same time the Andromeda was hit.'

I understood the significance of the android's conclusions. "You are saying the enemy's possible escape might have been hidden by the initial aftermath of the event?"

'I believe it to be probable. If they have escaped it will only be a matter of time before we face significant danger from the other two warships.'

Carla put two and two together. "We need to verify this but it will place the Andromeda at risk if they are playing possum."

'I have a solution for this dilemma, Mrs. Conroy. We keep the Andromeda at a safe distance while I use an EEP to make a quick visit to the warship.'

There five EEP's—Emergency Event pods—aboard the Andromeda, comprised of single occupant capsules which could evacuate personnel into space should anyone find themselves stranded after a general evacuation.

Sparkle continued. *'Being robotic AI I have no need for life support and will be able to move about the warship much more easily than a human. I also have significant military capability should any resistance be encountered. This also falls in line with the Robotic Code of Ethics and Conduct—to protect human life at all costs.'*

The android gaged the threat with accuracy and provided an equitable solution. The scheme made perfect sense. Everyone lapsed into a sober silence.

"I think it's an excellent suggestion, Sparkle. As much as I would hate to put you in harm's way I believe you will do a better job than any of us humans would be capable of."

As the President Commander of the Andromeda and chief executive of the mission it would have been within my right to make the decision but I looked to the flight crew for an evaluation of the proposed solution. They all nodded their heads in agreement.

"Is there anything you'll need, Sparkle—may I suggest a laser assault weapon?" Sparkle smiled. *'I will take the weapon but I have very effective lasers of my own, President Commander.'*

*

Twenty minutes later, with assault laser in hand the lieutenant squeezed into the EEP chosen for what we hoped would be a short mission. With the impetus provided by the Andromeda the capsule required a minimum thrust, to breach the distance between the two ships. The EEP took twenty-one minutes to make the journey. A view of developments from Sparkle's point of view displayed on the bridge's holo platform compliments of cameras within the android's eyes. Those not required to be at a service platform gathered around the receiver and we watched, like patrons of an old-time movie, but without the popcorn.

Sparkle gave us a running commentary of his progress. *'If you look at what appears to be the entrance, you will see an open hatch. This indicates the vessel has been depressurized—most unusual. There is significant damage to the propulsion area and I would think the inner hull has been breached by our missile. I am registering high radiation readings.'*

We watched with a mixed sense of enthrallment and foreboding as Sparkle maneuvered the capsule alongside the entrance and made contact with the hull of the warship. With secure magnetic docking the EEP stuck to the metallic outer-structure like the proverbial fly on a wall. The lieutenant released the canopy, unharnessed himself and clambered aboard plunging our video into darkness, until he turned on the twin spotlights, situated on each shoulder of his special EVA suit.

'I am detecting a very low current circulating in the heart of the ship somewhere. So far there appear to be no occupants—all cabins along this entrance hallway are empty and void of any items. This would be as a result of the depressurization.'

The android continued on until the passage-way broadened out into a large room with dozens of seats; perhaps a boardroom, of sorts. He swiveled around, showing the entire chamber before moving on to some steps and into another corridor. At the top of the landing three doorways became visible. The center door led to more steps and, I suspected, the nerve-center of the vessel. The doors on each side opened into smaller rooms and may have been used for storage.

'The origin of the low current detected earlier is closer now—I think we are approaching the bridge. The radiation levels are abnormally high and I believe everyone has already abandoned ship. Once the visual on their control room is completed it will be interesting to find out how they escaped.'

"My guess is they probably had an escape pod system, similar to ours. It could have been situated anywhere on board," I said.

'I will investigate, President Commander.'

The spotlights lit the main console of the bridge as the android crested the stairs. Dozens of alarm icons, switches, levers and gauges, festooned the main console. In the center, a screen took half the width of the cons and it struck me, their technology did not appear to be much different from our own.

The lieutenant's unemotional discourse continued. *'I have discovered the source of the low current, President Commander. I think we have a problem'.*

"What is it Sparkle?"

'It looks like a timing device of some sort. There is a small-gauge cable connecting it to what I think is a trigger device—it can only mean one thing.'

I went cold all over. Gary voiced my fears. "Shit, it may be a bomb set for intruders. They have escaped and have left the ship to be a death-trap for any boarding party."

In my heart I knew in to be true. "Get the fuck out of there, Sparkle. It could go off any second."

'I am leaving post-haste, President Commander. If I don't make it I have left an info-vial plugged into an auxiliary input on the bridge charging station. It contains an up-loadable program with the details of the Diamond 1000 processor. You will be able to supplement Mickey's programming with it.'

The video of the lieutenant's progress violently swiveled 180 degrees and we observed his headlong flight, down the steps to the passage-way that led back to the exterior hatch.

I am not a religious man but I prayed he would get out intact. Carla groaned in grief, the tears visible in her eyes and everyone gathered with us around the con, watched in dismay as the corridor lit up under the powerful beams of the spotlights. The android's exceptional speed capability would get it to the exit much faster than any human.

We waited as Sparkle streaked down the two sets of stairs and burst into the large chamber with all the seats, where he accelerated. Framed in the beams of light we could see the end of the passage-way and the exterior hatch.

"He's going to make it," I shouted.

Then the hologram dissolved into a fuzzy blackness.

"Mickey?"

'My sensors show there has been a huge explosion on the warship, President Commander.'

∞∞

Twenty-four

Sparkle is Lost

A palpable silence followed Mickey's announcement. For several minutes we stared at the empty holo-receiver and no one uttered a word.

Mickey's voice broke the silence. *'Prepare for shockwave—shields still at maximum strength.'*

The Andromeda's inner structures shrieked and groaned under the onslaught of compressed space as it smashed, without further warning, into the protective barrier around the hull. For the second time we endured a scary moment but it passed, much quicker than the first.

'No detectable damage to the Andromeda.' Sighs of relief broke out. Carla held onto me, with arms wrapped around my waist while I did my best to steady our swaying bodies.

"What about the lieutenant?" I asked.

After a short hesitation Mickey spoke, an emotion of sadness immanent in his normal impassive tone.

'I am sorry, President Commander. I do not detect the EEP at all—Lieutenant Sparkle's

processor has shut down and I believe he has been destroyed.'

Disbelief registered on the faces of the flight crew, some of whom uttered groans and gasps, unable to hide their shock. Carla raised a shaky hand to her mouth and stared at me with wide-open eyes. I wrapped my arms around her and attempted to digest the news. The realization dawned—androids are machines; assemblies of complex computers and circuitry and appeared sentient to us through the application of clever programs. Sparkle chose to investigate the derelict ship alone despite the inherent dangers of doing so and thereby fulfilled his mandate to preserve human life.

"Clear the Bridge please." I believed it expedient to return the crew to normal everyday procedures and allow everyone the opportunity to process the sudden loss of Lieutenant Sparkle. We also needed to assess a new danger: the likelihood of another visit from one, or both, of the remaining Crustan warships.

The crew left the bridge, some in earnest conversation and others deep in thought. The on-duty ensign remained at the con.

Gary broached the obvious. "I wonder how much time we have before the enemy arrives on our doorstep."

"I have no idea but one thing might work in our favor—the enormous distances and the time taken to travel from one position to another. The enemy might have near instantaneous communication but according to Ozzy's information, they're still subject to a maximum of 85 percent light-speed." I said.

"It's a pity no technological method is available to establish the whereabouts of the other warships," said Gary.

"Ozzy's intelligence gatherers alluded to the possibility of three prospecting vessels in the general area of Hera-soter. The same number of warships may indicate the pairing of military and prospecting disciplines. It would be fortuitous if the other two pairs found themselves in a different part of the galaxy."

Another six years of travel remained on the journey to our new planet—enough time for the enemy to intercept the Andromeda, from whatever position in space, their ships occupied.

Carla made a good point. "It will give us time to work on the anti-matter weapon."

Uncertain of the antimatter hypothesis time-line, my thoughts sought more immediate solutions. "I think we need to plan for imminent attack and hope for the best. We're several months away from having the new weapon ready—if they appear in the interim we will just need to handle it as efficiently as possible."

Gary reminded me of the lieutenant's last words. "We have a vial of the Diamond 1000 processor for uploading. I guess we better see to it immediately."

I agreed and walked to the charging station where the info-vial still remained plugged into an off-line port. I beckoned for Carla to follow me into the off-limits, main-frame room where all Mickey's hardware resided and placed the vial into a port.

"Mickey, your long awaited upgrade to the Diamond 1000 is on its way."

'Thank you, President Commander—it will be like having Lieutenant Sparkle back, in a way. I can already perceive my military awareness reaching new heights.'

"You will need every bit of its information if we run into the Crustans again."

*

Three years later: *2398 CE.*

Several years passed without any sign of the Crustans. We almost believed the destruction of the warship might have discouraged any further retaliation but deep within, I knew this could not be true. The enormous distances and limiting speeds of interstellar craft begged the possibility of a second encounter. If the crew of the destroyed enemy vessel escaped by means of emergency pods they would be sharing our story with the Crustan leaders at the first opportunity.

I assumed, with a FTL communication system, our existence would already be common knowledge to the enemy. Much depended on where the other two warships might be situated, so we maintained a constant vigil.

Ozzy visited the Andromeda on several more occasions. Our reunion, after the missile strike, brought everyone great pleasure and the alien voiced his praise to the flight crew. He congratulated all on their courage and paid condolences regarding Lieutenant Sparkle. As our destination drew closer we all sensed a growing fascination for our new home. The onboard planetarium, with its four-meter reflector telescope situated in the center of Andromeda City, became a popular venue for many of the ship's compliment, during their free time. The return to a normal life, in the wake of enemy confrontation, became a welcomed comfort for all.

*

"What nonsense have you been up to, Happydoo?"

My valet scrunched his eyes and raised a synthetic, upper lip in a wide grin, showing off his aesthetic teeth. The pirouette and foot-stomp routine followed—the predictable performance that telegraphed his irrepressible joy at an opportunity to be of service. The grin, however, disappeared the second his sideshow ended.

'My nonsense unfortunately carries a cautionary tale, Master Beckett.'

I decided to humor him. "Do tell, dear valet."

'The last clandestine snippet of information you left for our mysterious conspirator, appears to have garnered a reaction.'

Carla and I often talked about the altered hibernation protocols and our narrow escape from death, but for Happydoo's discovery. We needed to force the murderous SOB into the open, so Carla devised a plan; to offer some false information in the vicinity of a listening device.

"What sort of reaction are we talking about?"

'Remember your most recent snippet—a special communication on the day of the fire drill, Master Beckett?'

"The senior, safety supervisor's record—of one person who missed the drill? We added in a false record with the hope of soliciting some attention."

'It worked, Master Beckett. Someone on-board with IT authority accessed the record.'

"Do you have an IP? Is it traceable?"

'It came from a computer in the Fission Tech's office. The computer is used by the four

available techs, Laura Samuels being one of them, Master Beckett.'

I digested this information for a moment. Our suspicions of Laura's involvement, because of the accusation regarding the death of her husband, gained a little traction but my gut feel wanted to rule her out. Her recruitment, together with her husband's came long after the installation of the sign-in system for the master, flight-control computer. Then it dawned on me: Gary, being the XO of the Andromeda, checked over the propulsion section's incident report at the end of every shift. The recruitment of the other fission techs took place at the same time as Laura and her husband's; there appeared no real reason to suspect any of them but Gary Pearson, whose brother Colin worked on the installation, could be a prime suspect.

"Are Laura Samuels and the XO still seeing each other regularly?"

'They meet for lunch at the Bread Basket, Master Beckett. Apart from that I am not sure.'

"The XO is the only person involved with the fission department's computer who was present on the project at the time of Mickey's software installation. My intuition is telling me it has to be him. There might be a leadership motive—an aging man who needs to feel the glory of power of a full command. Have you shared any of this with Mrs. Carla?"

'Not yet, Master Beckett. I thought you would be the right person for that.'

Mickey's calm digital purr interrupted our conversation.

'President Commander to the bridge.'

I looked at Happydoo. Well done my friend —keep up the good work. We'll flush him out soon."

'I am happy to be of service, Master Beckett.'

I turned and made for the verticap. Out of the corner of my eye I saw the android do his little routine of appreciation triggered by the words of praise.

On my arrival at the bridge I found Gary waiting with folded arms and a look of deep concern on his face. Carla, involved with research in my office, heard Mickey's request for immediate attention and came to see what it entailed.

Gary indicated toward the trajectory screen. I could see the Andromeda depicted by a large icon. A dotted line extended out from the ship's position toward a small, red dot at the periphery of the screen.

"What is it, Mickey?"

We have an unidentified craft at the very edge of the heat sig-sensor range, President Commander.'

∞∞

Twenty-five

Mutiny

"What is the craft's velocity?"

'80 percent C, President Commander—it has to be a Crustan vessel.'

My heart sank under the weight of the potential confrontation and the hope of a trouble-free arrival at our destination evaporated.

"How long until we enter weapon's firing range?"

'Thirty-three minutes, President Commander. I will initiate protective shields on detection of any hostile action.'

"Better send out the warning immediately—everyone is to make for the escape pods. Prime the two forward anti-matter guns for action and keep them on notice. We'll use our nukes first.

Gripped by the tenseness of the moment, everyone managed to remain calm. Half-an-hour later, with our eyes glued to the red icon on the screen, we watched the dotted line between the Andromeda and the Enemy warship begin to diminish. Then, something happened to surprise us —a few seconds before entering firing range, the red icon changed course.

"What the fuck are they doing?" Gary spluttered.

We watched the enemy's trajectory change from head-on confrontation to the execution of a wide arc, before swinging back to cross behind us —a similar move made by the first warship. Half an hour later, the enemy, having completed the maneuver came around on our port side, flying a parallel course to our own.

Carla spoke for the first time. "Do you think they're going to come alongside us like the first warship did?"

"I somehow doubt it," I said. "They must know we sent the first ship to oblivion. All we can expect from them is a fusillade of nukes."

'The warship has taken up a position out of firing range and has slowed down to match our velocity.'

Gary stroked his short beard. "My guess is they are too chicken to take us on alone—they're waiting for the other ship to arrive. Only God knows how long that will be."

Gary's comment seemed feasible. The three enemy ships might have gone in different directions with their respective prospecting vessels. This ship might have been closer to our position than the third warship, the arrival which may be many hours, days or even months away—a lengthy period to wait.

"We need to keep a constant vigil in case they make a sudden move—in the meantime we can send the people back to their stations with instructions to remain ready," I said. "Mickey, maintain weapon's readiness—we'll just have to wait this out."

'Weapons will remain ready, Boss. I will inform you of any change in the warship's position. Diamond 1000 program is now fully installed in my processor. There is a combat protocol based on an enemy's movement and weapon firing sequences. Would you like me to execute engagement on immediate hostility, or do I wait for your command?'

"If I don't answer your execution request within five seconds, be my guest, Mickey."

'Your instruction is duly noted, President Commander.'

*

The third warship must have been a great distance away. After three weeks the second vessel made no change to its position and we became accustomed to the presence. Everyone continued on with their regime, leaving the vigilance to Mickey's acute sensor capabilities.

One morning, while busy with reports I heard the slight whirring noise made by an android in the process of folding its arms. The sound broke my intense concentration and I glanced up, startled by the intrusion.

"You wanted a word, Happydoo?"

'Yes please, Master Beckett. I believe I have discovered further evidence regarding the plot to remove you from leadership.'

"You have my undivided attention."

'It involves all the auto-bots on the ship. A specific line of code which will counter their standing instructions has been recently added to the maintenance program under the guise of new lubricants and joint adjustments.'

"Who authorized it?"

'It has not been authorized and when I approached Chief Spanner, the android in charge of all the ship's technical maintenance, he denied any knowledge of it.

"What does the code call for?"

'It instructs all maintenance-bots to seal off the propulsion area and subdue any human effort to prevent this from coming about, Master Beckett. The security-bots are to seal off the bridge and all entrances leading up to flight control from Andromeda City.'

"Do you have any idea who might have initiated the plan?"

'Not conclusively, Master Beckett but the code reveals a call-sign to be acknowledged by the bots—it's two zeros, preceded by two letters—

XPoo. The bots are to take instruction from anyone bearing this marker. '

"The propulsion area and the bridge both
have independent control functions by which
communication with the Master Flight Computer
can be severed. Mickey would have no jurisdiction
and whoever has control of these two areas would
be in charge of the ship."

'I believe we need to act immediately Master Beckett. If Chief Spanner is in on the plot he
already knows we are on to it.'

The sudden blaring of an alarm shrieked its
audible tyranny throughout Andromeda. The
blood almost froze in my veins as I struggled to
gather my wits. The first thought to enter my mind
alluded to a possible change in the enemy warship's status but it dispelled; the sound of the
alarm did not indicate an emergency. In the event
the Crustans made a move Mickey would initiate
an emergency throughout the entire vessel. The
sound in question emanated from the Con and im-
plied the sudden lockdown of a specific area.

Happydoo and I scuttled out of the office in
haste toward the bridge but as we approached the
steps, leading to the main console, two maintenance-bots stepped into our path and prevented
further progress. Happydoo stepped in front of me
but the maintenance-bot extended one of its arms
to knock him off his feet. The speed and accuracy
of the bot's action astounded me. Poor old Happy-

doo sprawled into the wall of the corridor in a tangle of arms and legs. I stood still as the bot approached, expecting to be slung aside but it stopped short, the blue beam of its single rectangular sensor, situated on top of the short, stocky frame oscillating back and forth like an old fashioned lighthouse. Then its digital voice spoke.

'Do not move, President Commander. You are under arrest.'

My astonishment knew no bounds. "Who gave you this order?" I asked.

'XPoo gave the order, President Commander.'

Now my anger surfaced. "And who the fuck is XPoo?"

The bot stepped aside and I could see the Con. Gary Pearson stood there, a half-smile on his face.

"I am XPoo, Beckett. But you already knew that," Pearson answered.

"You can't do this, Gary."

"On the contrary—I can do what I like. You may have discovered the little plan we set to eliminate you and your troublesome spouse but I have you over a barrel now."

"What motivated you to commit mutiny, Pearson. This obviously started a long time ago—before we left the mining venture and joined the Habitat Program."

"In deed it did, President Commander. It started when you inherited the corporation from your uncle. When he was in charge I commanded the Andromeda—he saw to the business of mining. When you arrived I smelled trouble from the beginning because he had such a soft spot for you. When you took over you I was relegated to second in charge."

"So...you're a bitter, aging commander who feels he has missed the boat."

The XO laughed. "I didn't miss the boat, Beckett—you stole it from me."

"It was never yours to take. My uncle worked his ass off to build the mining venture while you were struggling through the ranks. He saw some potential in you and gave you an opportunity and now you are usurping something which doesn't belong to you."

"Fuck your sanctimonious arrogance. Spare me the moral speech, Beckett. I saw my chance to be the one who would spearhead this project and I took it. My brother helped and he will be on one of the future vessels that leave Earth for Hera-soter."

"What do you intend to do with me, Pearson?"

"I would think it to be obvious. You and your wife have to be eliminated—I will see to this aspect of the plan in a day or two. I am not alone. There are eleven disgruntled crew members who see me as the real leader and soon, the entire ship's company will acknowledge me as the new President Commander."

"You're a fucking idiot if you think you can get away with this, Pearson."

"Just watch me. Your fate is sealed and any resistance would be futile."

Pearson turned to the two maintenance-bots. "Take him to the brig. There is to be no food or water given—they won't be needing it."

The two bots grabbed me, one on each side and their three-pronged fingers bit into my flesh like vice-grips. I yelled out in pain but they took no heed and hauled me off my feet toward the verti-cap.

"Now let's see what the great, President Commander Conroy, can do," said Pearson.

His mocking voice rang in my ears as I passed out from the pain in my arms.

∞∞

Twenty-six

Incarcerated

Ten minutes later I regained consciousness. Carla's tearful eyes stared into mine with deep concern as she sat on the floor with my head cradled in her hands. I could see her lips moving but could not hear the words in my semi-conscious state. It took a few minutes for me to surface through the fog and clear my head with sufficient focus to take stock of our surroundings. I tried to sit but Carla cautioned me. Blood oozed from the wounds on both arms as she tried to wipe the punctured flesh with the sleeve of her flight-suit.

"Take it easy, Hon—you're bleeding—try not to move around."

Her voice calmed my emotions . Movement exacerbated the pain, so I complied without being my usual difficult self.

"How long have you been in here, Sweetheart?" I asked.

"They brought me in five minutes before you. Two server-bots confronted me and escorted me to the cell—what's this all about?"

I told her. When Carla understood the precariousness of our situation she became quiet as she gave thought to possible solutions.

"You said Happydoo discovered the present plot but there had been no time to anything?"

"Yes, we were discussing it when the alarm went off. I didn't understand what was happening at first, but the bridge area had been sealed off by the two maintenance-bots."

"What happened to Happydoo?"

I thought for a moment. "It's funny. He had been knocked aside by one of the bots but I don't recall seeing him when they dragged me off the bridge area."

She wiped away some beads of perspiration from my forehead with her fingers. "Do you remember the time when you and Uncle Sid's secretary, what was her name again?—

"Freda," I answered.

"—that's right, Freda—it was in that factory you were investigating and the WGF security team was killed?"

I nodded my head. "Could I ever forget?"

"Well, the point is—it was Happydoo who save you and Freda."

I looked into her beautiful, emerald eyes and for a brief moment the redness from the tears seemed to evaporate, giving way to a glimmer of hope.

"You mean if he has escaped the bots and is in hiding somewhere?"

"Exactly. It is entirely possible he's already planning to help us."

As bleak as the situation appeared I knew Happydoo, if still un-apprehended and in one piece, would make a plan to free us. With sudden optimism my sprit leapt in anticipation and we smiled at each other.

*

Twenty four hours passed without any visitors—hunger and thirst posed a problem for both of us but at least the pain from my wounds, diminished to an acceptable level.

"I wonder who the other eleven people are?" Carla mused.

"I bet Laura Samuels is one of the number. I can't even begin to guess who else might be involved."

"How much time do you think we have, Hon?"

"Pearson mentioned I would be in the brig for a day or two. He specifically instructed the bots do make sure I wasn't fed or given anything to drink—said I wouldn't need it."

"But, he did say we would both be eliminated?"

"That's what he said—I think he is trying to cook up a plan to make our disappearance look like an accident. That way, the rest of the ship's compliment won't ask any questions and he can take over, without any drama."

Carla huddled against me on the narrow bench. "I wonder where Happydoo is?"

"It's no use worrying about it, Sweetheart. He'll come, if he's able—I know it."

We heard Gary Pearson's voice several times over the ship's general com. A speaker, about twenty meters from the brig's door, provided us with audio of any announcements intended for the flight crew. The brig, situated in the bowels of the vessel and a place few people ever needed to be, explained the absence of ship's personnel. With each broadcast I tried to decipher the conspirator's future plans and speculate on what they might have in store for us. The brig sported an occupant-sensor which would keep Mickey informed of our location. All personnel carried an injected chip that revealed identity and vital signs—not much help to us in the present predicament. The Master Flight Computer would obey the commands of any executive crew member who constituted the ship's final authority—Carla, Pearson, the on-duty ensign and myself. My neural transmitter, which lay in our sleeping quarters, left me with no way to contact Mickey and I chided myself for tardiness. The transmitter should form part of my regular dress code. On Earth, regular com stations for AI contact did not exist everywhere, but the ship provided these stations in many places. This made use of the neural-transmitter on the Andromeda unnecessary.

The com blared to life again and I heard Mickey's calm, silky purr.

'I have two questions for you, Lieutenant Commander Pearson.'

"Shoot, Mickey."

'Why are President Commander and Mrs. Conroy in the brig.'

I perceived Mickey now knew about our incarceration.

"The President Commander and Mrs. Conroy are in breach of certain security code, Mickey. Their incarceration became necessary for a limited period."

'What security code breach would that be, Lieutenant Commander?'

I liked the direction of the conversation. The AI needed to question the veracity of such a decision. It also meant the entire ship's crew would hear it—perhaps this fact escaped our mutinous XO's mind.

Many of the crew loved Carla and I. They considered us to be almost parental in their lives. I am sure they would love to know the details of this transgression. For shit's sake, what could a leader do to earn such legal action?

Pearson didn't answer the question but repeated himself, and then added: "I need to inform the ship's crew of the matter. I do not want to discuss this over the com."

I smirked at Carla. "Now he's put his foot in it. There will be questions from the crew."

She agreed. The AI posed another question.

'Why has my control of the propulsion and flight-control systems been terminated?'

Pearson didn't answer right away but took his time. I suspected he couldn't think of a valid reason to have locked Mickey out.

The AI became impatient. *'Lieutenant Commander—due to the action an anomaly has arisen in my reasoning and logic parameters. It will cause a problem with my handling of any future emergencies.'*

Pearson's answer reflected on his ability to handle unforeseen situations. "I don't really give a shit, Mickey. I have taken over control because there are things that need to be done without your interference—you'll just have to suck it up."

'I do not understand these expressions, Lieutenant Commander but I take it you are usurping the President Commander's leadership and voiding my ability to protect the Andromeda from enemy attacks.'

If Pearson thought his mutiny would be straight forward the scales might now be falling from his eyes with some alacrity. Not being military-minded he would need Mickey and the Diamond 1000 war component or we would all be done for.

Backed into a corner he conceded. "I understand we need your expertise should the warship attack us and I will return control back to you in the event they make a move. Your mandate is to protect the Andromeda and its crew—which includes me and collaborators, but until it happens I must retain full control."

'Very well, Lieutenant Commander Pearson. I have nothing further to say on the matter.'

*

Thankful for Mickey's intrusion on Pearson's plans to usurp my authority Carla and I discussed the issue at length. With the obvious mutiny now broadcasted throughout the entire ship at least everyone would be aware of the predicament. My hope still rested in Happydoo to launch some sort of rescue attempt. He would have access to Mickey's expertise and between them a plan of action would be formed for our rescue.

Four hours later the status quo changed, but not for the better. Mickey's voice floated through the Com:

'All flight crew to their respective stations—Andromeda City occupants to the escape

pods; third enemy warship approaching—I need immediate access to all systems, Lieutenant Commander Pearson.'

∞∞

Twenty-seven

Dealing with the Insurrection

Carla shot me a frightened glance. Fear of the potential confrontation registered in her eyes and words of comfort failed me. She clung to me and smothered her face into my neck—her body trembled against mine in anticipation of the Crustan attack.

A brief moment of relief followed when the com blared to life again and Pearson, in a subdued voice uttered, "Control of Main com and propulsion area is back in your hands, Mickey. Please direct anticipated actions to me and wait for clearance."

The AI made a statement which I attributed to the new Diamond 1000 program. A measure of independence highlighted Mickey's new military awareness.

'I am afraid I can only share the command decision procedure with the appointed President Commander. Under the hibernation protocols the leadership was invested in you while President Commander Conroy remained in stasis. No clear instruction of your promotion to the lead position

exists at this time—therefore I reserve the right to take full command of the vessel.'

Pearson objected strongly. "I cannot return fucking control of the vessel if you refuse to acknowledge my leadership."

'The choice is yours, Lieutenant, Commander—however, if you do not hand over the control to me I cannot protect the Andromeda—there will be no protective shields or weapon deployment. We will all be doomed.'

Silence reigned for a moment as the XO considered his options. Then he relented.

"Very well, you fucking conglomeration of wires and circuits. I'll relinquish the control but you had better keep us safe."

'Thank you, Lieutenant Commander. Prepare for conflict. I would suggest you make for your designated escape pod and remain there until I say it is safe to return.'

Carla and I listened for more dialog but no further objections came from Pearson. Mickey now took full control of the ship and all its systems. We both sighed in relief and sat on the bench again, to await the inevitable. At least with Mickey in control we stood a chance of survival. A soft sound, the whir of AI gadgetry, caught our attention and we glanced toward the brig's entrance to take in a welcome sight.

'Have you and Mrs. Carla had enough together-time, Master Beckett?'

Happydoo stood there with folded arms, a huge grin creased the synthetic skin around his mouth. Our consternation gave way to joy.

"I've never been happier to see you, you digital bucket of bolts and wires—I can only imagine the nonsense you've been up to while we've been locked away in here."

The android, again as on previous occasions, performed the pirouette and foots-stomp routine. His smile widened into the widest Cheshire grin he could muster from the intrepid program within his quantum processor brain. He tapped on the exterior keypad, the brig's force barrier released and we stepped out into the corridor to savor our freedom.

"Is there really a threat from a third warship?" I asked.

Happydoo gave us his most mischievous look. The corners of his lips curled upwards, into part smirk and part grin.

'Mickey and I made that up. I managed to escape those two maintenance bots and secure a connection to the Master Control motherboard from the storage area, where Ossimantus's Orbitron is parked during his visits. Mickey and I evolved a plan to beat Mr. Pearson at his own game. He is not a very bright man.'

We listened in astonishment. Happydoo showed wisdom beyond his programming and I wondered if the programmers hit on a type of sentience to creep into his digital mind over a period of time. The NWE AI programming profession's goal, at the time of Happydoo's most recent upgrade before we left Earth, focused much of their effort on this aspect. Could such an inclusion have been made in my valet's case?

'Your XO is at present holed up in an empty, escape pod, Master Beckett. I have instructed Mickey to lock it so he cannot escape, or contact any bots.'

I embraced the indomitable android around the shoulders. His intuitiveness and ingenuity saved my bacon once again—I felt deeply grateful to him.

"What about his league of bots and the other humans who have pledged allegiance to him?"

'The XO cannot have any contact with anyone at the moment, Master Beckett. I have written a new program for the bots, overriding the command Mr. Pearson gave them but we can't be sure they will obey it. As to the humans who are on his side we may never know for sure unless we can find one who in turn will turn the others in.'

"Or her," interjected Carla.

'You are referring to Laura Samuels, Mrs. Carla?'

"I am," she said.

'We do not know for certain if she is involved, Mrs. Carla. If we approach her she will

certainly deny it and we have no way of proving her complicity.'

Happydoo made a good point. I considered our options while we walked toward the bridge-bound verticap.

"So, nobody else is in the escape pods at the moment?"

'We released everyone after the XO entered his pod, Master Beckett. I detailed security with the arrangement and they saw to it once Mr. Pearson entered the pod, he was detained and the rest sent back to their stations.'

"I bet he was extremely unhappy about being taken in, and by two AI's, at that."

'His language was incomprehensible, Master Beckett—we strapped him into his compression couch to await a court martial.'

The Andromeda did not operate on a military basis, however, the more I thought about the action, the more I liked it.

"We need to find out if the bots will obey the new code you wrote. Can we get through to the armory from here without running in to any of them?"

'I believe there is a way, Master Beckett—if you and Mrs. Carla will follow me.'

The android led us away from the verticap station, toward a door near the entrance to the crew's private canteen. Not all entrances operated with a force barrier and this one I knew to be an emergency escape stairwell, used in a case of possible verticap failure. He opened the door and we scuttled through onto the landing. The stairwell lights, which operated on the emergency system offered a dim illumination as we descended the double helix-styled steps to the armory.

We arrived at another door on the lowest level and Happydoo indicated for us to wait. He opened the door a crack and peeped out into the corridor.

'There is a maintenance bot standing in the armory entrance, Master Beckett. I can also see the armory ensign sitting at her desk.'

"The ensign is more than likely a prisoner. If she moves the bot will kill her—we must distract it somehow," I said.

'I will act as decoy, Master Beckett. First I will see if the bot will obey me under the new code permission number. If not, then I will try to get it to chase me and you can slip in to speak to the ensign and secure a hand-laser.'

I nodded my approval. "Be careful, Happydoo. Don't allow the bot to get too close to you."

'Fortunately I am much faster, Master Beckett. I will try to get it to move away from the entrance, so you will have to be very quick in obtaining the weapon.'

"Let's get going, then," I answered.

The android half-opened the door and stepped through into the corridor—obscured from the bot's view Carla and I peeped around the jamb to gain a view. As we waited Happydoo caught the bot's attention with a whistle. It swiveled at the sound and the curved visor, which concealed the movement sensor beam, swiveled from side to side in an attempt to identify the intruder.

The android issued a terse command. *'XP01 commands you to stand down and allow me to pass.'*

The bot responded. *'Command protocol sign-number is not recognized.'*

It moved forward to threaten Happydoo.

He didn't wait and launched himself at the bot in a mock charge but stopped short of the sphere of its physical contact ability. The bot responded with its one arm and took a swipe in the android's direction. It lurched forward in an attempt to close in on him but Happydoo moved with the swiftness of a deer. He backed off, and turned to move further along the corridor, away from us. At the same time he gestured with his hand—I think he must have learned the sign from my father—and gave the finger. The tenseness of the situation negated a potential smile but under different circumstances I would have collapsed in laughter. The bot lurched forward again and screeched a command in a high-pitched voice. *'You are in breach of XP00 command, android, Happydoo. Stop and submit to my instructions.'*

Happydoo laughed allowed and continued to back away. The bot followed with repeated commands until it came within three feet of the android, to lung with its mechanical arm in a swiping-motion, again. I flinched at the sight of the bot's speed and agility but it could not match its target's maneuverability.

Carla shoved me from behind. "Let's go, Beckett. Before it turns and sees us."

∞∞

Twenty-eight

Maintenance Bot AM11

On Carla's prompt I overcame my sudden mental inertia. We scuttled across the corridor, into the entrance of the armory where the wide-eyed ensign sat at the desk, her face a picture of surprise.

"Quickly, Ensign—grab me a heavy caliber laser—I need to neutralize that bot."

The ensign sprang into action and ran to the glassed-door, weapon case against the wall of the armory and keyed in a code. It took a few seconds before the door opened to allow her entry for the removal of a long-stock laser rifle with the firing key. I grabbed the weapon she thrust in my direction and heard the sound of the bot's tracks, followed by Carla's sudden gasp of fear. While still in the process of weapon-lock release, I turned to look at my adversary and it caused me to fumble the safety catch. To make matters worse my arm caught on the corner of the cabinet door and a sharp pain coursed through my nervous system. The bot, already inside the armory, towered over Carla, its mechanical arm already raised for a swipe at her. A direct hit from its pincers would dislodge her head.

I yelled out to Carla to fall flat on the ground and clicked off the laser safety. My hope rested in Carla's instant reaction—I should not have been concerned with regard to her reflexes and instincts—she already anticipated my move. The power surge from the laser caught the bot high on the shoulder and diminished the arms impetus for a brief moment. It shook and reeled to one side as the shot caused havoc with prime circuitry. A more central shot would be required to neutralize the bot's processor. Carla rolled over to get away from the AI's tracks as it slithered along toward me, its beam of purple-blue light in a wild oscillation. I fired again and caught it in the middle of the torso. A great belch of smoke poured from the processor's panel-cover, as the bot teetered over me with arm raised high in the air, in a desperate attempt to make contact. One more shot from the laser hit the upper segment of the bot's arm as it swung the mechanical arm in the direction of my head. The intended blow at my cranium missed and the pincers struck the glass door of the weapon cabinet. Shards of glass shot in all directions. I saw Carla move away toward the entrance behind the bot, in an effort to escape erratic flails of both arms.

The ensign stood routed to the spot, paralyzed by fear. A young woman, with limited experience, she would be chopped liver if I didn't stop the AI. I could see its visor swiveling toward her and zone in on her position—the beam enveloped her frame. The huge arm, blackened from my first strike rose into the air again, in preparation of a death blow. The ensign shrieked, fainted in sheer terror at the horrific sight and crumbled to the ground in a heap. This final involuntary act saved her life.

The bot swung the huge metal arm toward her but the pincers on the end caught the ledge of the weapon's cabinet. This fortunate stroke of luck reduced the severity of the blow and redirected the arm's aim, to hit the counter behind the ensign's unconscious body. At the same time, I maneuvered behind the bot to get off a shot to finalize the hapless AI's demise. The shot hit it in the central-back area where all its circuitry passed through a conduit to the processor, and severed all its vital connections. A plume of acrid smoke rose to the armory ceiling and the robot went limp, stopped on its tracks, mere inches from the ensign. A sudden surge of relief flooded my being.

"Are you okay, Hon?" Carla asked.

"I'm good," I answered. "I hope the ensign is alright, though."

Carla moved around the neutralized automaton and bent down over the ensign, feeling her jugular. "She's going to be okay—just passed out from fright."

Happydoo stood at the entrance to peer in at the scene, satisfaction written all over his synthetic features. *'Well done, Master Beckett. It looks like maintenance-bot AM11 will not be operating any time soon.'*

"Your instruction overwriting didn't work, Happydoo. Do you know how many bots are involved and is there any other way we can neutralize them without this type of destruction?"

'That is a question we will have to ask Mickey, Master Beckett. Now that there is no more conflict with his protocols it should be possible to find a way.'

The ensign awoke from her fainting spell and sat up with Carla's help. It took her a few minutes to gain total lucidity, before she could speak.

"I was so frightened, President Commander. This terrible maintenance bot barged into my office and told me to remain still or I would be harmed. I heard the final broadcasted conversation between Lieutenant Commander Pearson and the Master Control Computer—I felt conflicted—I knew something was wrong."

We explained Pearson's attempted mutiny and appeased her concerns regarding the future. I instructed her to close off the armory to prevent any other robot from entering and asked her to remain inside until further notice. We still needed to neutralize the threat posed by the rest of Pearson's compliment. We left her in the hope she would be able to cope.

I considered our options. "We need to get to a reporting station and have a word with Mickey," I said.

The three of us trooped off, back to the emergency stairs below the bridge deck. An input station, opposite the verticap would serve our purpose, but we needed to be vigilant. The possibility of rogue bots remained a threat. The corridor at the verticap station appeared peaceful and we took the opportunity to contact Mickey.

"Mickey, this is the President Commander. Thank you for the way you handled that serious situation with the XO."

'It is my pleasure, Boss. Welcome back to command.'

"Do you know how many bots are still under the XO's code of mutiny—is there a way we can neutralize them without a fight?"

'There are four maintenance bots and six server-bots involved, President Commander. The only member to receive Happydoo's rewritten code appears to be Chief Spanner. I see you have already dealt with one of the maintenance bots— this leaves three plus the six servers. There is a way to deal with them but they will be absent from any type of useful service until each one is individually reprogrammed by manual means.'

I gave this some consideration. "That shouldn't be a problem in the short term. I will get my valet to reprogram each one afterwards. What is it you can do from your end?"

''I can enter a conflicting code dynamic which will cause an anomaly in their service protocol—this is very similar to the anomaly the XO posed to my rationale by trying to usurp your command without the correct clearance.'

"Very well, Mickey. Go ahead and do it. Please supply Happydoo with the clearance code so he can manually correct the damage done by XPoo. Let me know when the bots have been neutralized."

'Will do, Boss. I know this is going to sound strange, almost like a real emotion, but I'm very technologically happy to have you back in the driving seat.'

"Thanks, Mickey. I appreciate your consideration – resulting from a real emotion, though."

Carla laughed and slapped me on the shoulder, while Happydoo went into the foot-stomp routine. We decided to sneak into the crew's canteen and help ourselves to cafteen from the meal replicator.

My next action would be to deal with my XO, a task I did not look forward to. Gary Pearson and I went back many years and it saddened me to think on our past friendship. Forgiveness could not be considered due to the severity of the crime.

Gary's greed, to take the command away from me —a selfish desire, which drove him to consider murder, paved the way for his own demise—the leopard never changes its spots. This treasonable offense weighed on my conscience and I still needed to contemplate the options.

∞∞

Twenty-nine

The Third Warship

Days, turned into weeks and weeks into months. Four months later the problem of an imminent attack still haunted everyone and it became difficult to keep one's composure. The second warship still shadowed us, outside of our weapon's range and never once altered velocity or position. The threat of the third warship's appearance compounded this position—how long would it take for them to arrive on our doorstep? Gary Pearson, my mutinous XO languished in the brig and a suitable punishment for his crime still eluded me.

The bot incident resolved itself after Mickey's intervention and Happydoo's reprogramming mission to break the mutinous XP00 code and rendered all fit for duty again. We could not, however, allow ourselves to become complacent with the status quo and I continued to exhort all the flight personnel to be ready for change.

At a time least expected, our situation took a precipitous turn.

*

"President Commander to the Bridge."

The request came from the on-duty ensign at the Con which brought a rude interruption to our sleep period. At first, the words didn't register in my fuzzy, dream-filled mind and Carla placed her hand on my shoulder to give it a shake.

"Shit. It can only mean one of two things," I mumbled.

"Come on, Hon let's get dressed," said Carla.

Five minutes later we both stood at the main console to stare at the holo-receiver platform. A hologram of the space-time ahead showed a slow fusion of photons, to produce a shadow-image of an object in travel toward us at high velocity. There could be no mistaking its identity—the third Crustan warship.

The on-duty ensign made a comment. "I detect a surge of power in the cargo hold, President Commander."

A tap on my shoulder turned out to be an excited Happydoo.

"What is it, Happydoo?"

'The alien, Ossimantus has just arrived, Master Beckett. The Orbitron is parked in the usual place.'

This news explained the power surge in the cargo hold. The visit from our good friend, Ozzy, did much to boost my morale.

"Bring him straight to the bridge when he's ready," I said.

The android turned and left the bridge. I knew Ozzy's visit would be brief as he could not afford to be aboard the Andromeda and risk damage to his Orbitron, when we came under attack. His presence suggested there might be something important for me to know regarding the immediate future and I looked forward to speaking with him.

"Speak to me, Mickey."

'The warship is still sixty-eight light-minutes away, President Commander. They are closing at 80% C so we can expect them to arrive within weapon's range in forty-two minutes.'

"Is there any change in our shadow's position?"

'Not at this time, Boss.'

"I am leaving the details of this coming battle in your capable hands, Mickey. May the force, in this case the Diamond 1000, be with you."

'All nuclear weapons are primed and awaiting instruction, President Commander—I will do my best. All Andromeda's compliment is being sent to the escape pods as we speak. Please take to your compression couches in your designated pods. What do you want to do with Mr. Pearson, Boss?'

"Have two of the security bots release him from the brig and incarcerate him in his designated pod, Mickey. I can't risk him being placed in a pod at this time. Make sure he is secured and inform the pod's security officer."

I turned to Carla and embraced her. "Go quickly to our escape pod, Sweetheart. I need to meet with Ozzy—I know he'll not be able to remain and there is possibly something important he wants me to know."

She held me tight for a few moments and broke away for the escape pod. The on-duty ensign excused himself and left the bridge, which left me alone at the Con. I waited for another minute before I saw Happydoo step out of the verticap, with Ozzy trailing on behind.

"Greetings my dear Earthling friend," he said. "I know this is not a good time for any of us but I wanted to bring you something."

"You no doubt know the third warship is about to arrive so I hope you have some good news for me."

Ozzy did his usual air-pressure differential thing and the huge, single eye, oscillated a few times.

"You have the weapons to defeat them, however, they are a force to be reckoned with. Destroying one on its own is a feat in its self—do not underestimate their battle intelligence. I want to give you a device which you will need to keep on you at all times."

The alien handed me a necklace with an oval-shaped object dangling from the center. It looked like a large, shiny medal, worn by many of our military generals back on Earth.

"This is not what you think it is. If you look carefully at the center piece of the object you will see it turns when pressure is applied. All you have to do is to turn it 360 degrees—one complete twist should do it."

I experimented and the knob-like center turned with ease. "This is great, Ozzy, but what does it do?"

Again the single eye ogled me for a brief moment. "If you are in a really tight spot and you have to evacuate the Andromeda—I'm not implying this will happen—I'm merely saying, if......this instrument will send out your coordinates in code and I will always be able to find you."

"So it's like a GPS of sorts?" I said.

Ozzy bobbed several times. "Yes—exactly. It's called a Universal Distress Signal Transmitter."

Although pleased at the alien's thoughtfulness I sensed he might have experienced a lack of confidence in our ability to overcome the two enemy ships.

"You think we might lose this battle?" I asked.

"I have every confidence in your AI and its Diamond 1000 military smarts but I am simply preparing for every eventuality."

I gave him a wry smile. "Thank you, Ozzy. I'll keep the transmitter hanging around my neck at all times but I believe we can beat the Crustan menace."

He bobbed again and released compressed air. "That's the right attitude, my friend—I must get going. I will see you in the near future."

"Sure Ozzy, look after yourself."

I looked at Happydoo. "Please see Ossimantus back to the Orbitron. I am going to stay here, at the con."

Happydoo gave me a sideways glance. 'Mrs. Carla is going to be very unhappy with you, Master Beckett.'

"I know, but my place is at the helm—even if Mickey is in charge. Please tell Mrs. Carla it has to be this way and I will see her when the fight is over."

I strapped myself into the compression couch and watched them leave the bridge.

"It's all in your hands now, Mickey. Do us all proud," I said.

'I will do my best President Commander. For the record—staying at the con is against the emergency protocol but I understand your logic. I will keep you updated as we progress.'

∞∞

Thirty

Malfunction

Interminable minutes passed as we waited for the third warship to enter range. Thirty minutes later the second ship made a sudden change in trajectory and rocketed upward at a sixty degree angle. Mickey turned on the holo-receiver so I could follow both ship's movements. I remembered that the translation device Ozzy gave us to make contact with the Crustans on the previous encounter could still play a part if I chose to do so. It now straddled the frame of my compression couch and the flick of a switch would put me in contact with the Crustan vessel's overseers.

Mickey, however, circumvented my thoughts before I could act.

'Missiles have been launched from both enemy vessels simultaneously—1.2 light-minutes from first impact. Preparing nukes and bringing antimatter canons to bear—firing four nukes and targeting third warship with anti-matter canon. Missiles away! Antimatter cannons malfunction— applying counter-measure maneuver and deploying intercept flares— raising protective shields against enemy missile impact.'

"What the fuck has happened to the anti-matter cannons, Mickey? We desperately need those in this fight."

'It would appear there is a glitch in the priming system, Boss. I am trying to find a way around it but I have to raise the shields to fend off the enemy strikes.'

"Understood. Can you dispatch a maintenance bot to see what the glitch is?"

'Already initiated, President Commander—intercept flares ineffective—prepare for missile impact.'

"I realize we can't fire missiles while our protective shields provide protection for the hull, but the antimatter canon's specific purpose is to deal with the enemy before their incoming missiles strike us. All we can throw at them now are more nukes?" I questioned.

'I am afraid this is true—until anti-matter cannons are primed and ready, they are useless to us.'

I waited for an eternity. The stench of fear ingrained in my sweat, wafted into my nostrils. When the impact came it shook the Andromeda from stern to bow. Alarms blared out, toxic messages and a myriad of lights festooned the con. The perspiration poured into my eyes as I released the grip on one side of the couch to drag a hand over my brow. The ship listed to port for a few moments before Mickey made a correction to bring it back on even keel again.

'Prepare for second missile strike. Shadow vessel now twenty light-minutes, directly above the Andromeda.'

My heart sank. We would be fortunate to survive the first strike—now a second salvo threatened to complicate matters.

"Any luck with the antimatter canons, Mickey?"

'Working on it, Boss.'

The shriek of alarms created a weird symphony of urgency and I did my best to check out terminated services represented by these lights but the couch straps made it difficult. Our internal gravity appeared to be zero and the main lighting extinguished. The emergency lights flickered on to trigger a ghost-like illumination of the con and bridge structure. It brought back the awful memory of the attack by the first Crustan vessel, before we dispatched it to alien Valhalla.

The second strike came and shook the superstructure worse than the first. A sudden struggle for breathable air indicated the loss of pressure in the vessel.

Mickey issued the pressure status with his usual calm purr. *'We are losing air pressure, Boss —unstrap yourself and get over to the EVA cabinet—you will die without a suit.'*

I needed no further incentive. EVA suits for this type of emergency were situated off to my left, a few feet from the con. With the straps undone it took a few seconds for the lack of gravity to make its presence known and I floated off in the wrong direction. A quick grab at the corner of the main con to maneuver my body in the right direction took some effort.

The journey to the EVA cabinet took a few more seconds and by the time I arrived, my lungs required extra oxygen, which I attained with great gulps from the disappearing breathable atmosphere. To open the cabinet door and remove an EVA suit took an even greater effort. By the time I managed to don the suit and return to the safety of the couch, perspiration poured over my forehead onto my face, within the confine of the EVA. All sound disappeared and I switched on my suit comm.

"Speak to me, Mickey."

His steady, digital purr tickled my eardrums. 'Glad to see you made the EVA cabinet, Boss—you had me worried for a second.'

Again, as with Happydoo and the maintenance bot situation, I would have laughed but the circumstances could not evoke my humor. I couldn't imagine the AI worried about any particular circumstance—or could a type of artificial, cyber-anxiety have come with inheritance of the Diamond 1000 system? My mind cleared away these fine thoughts and reinstated my composure. I think I came close to an attack of shit-pants through the duration of the enemy strikes. The escape pods, with their own supply of gravity, plus air-pressure control, could survive on their own.

'The Hull is breached in two places, President Commander—initiating sealing of area H-405 and H-611. Internal Hull reseal-bots locked in and shell fracture repair has begun.'

Two breaches constituted a serious problem for hull integrity. By the area numbers the breaches, one on the starboard side near the main city recreational area and one on top close to the center of the roof, might pose a threat to the remainder of the pods. I hoped to God these pods escaped critical damage or complete destruction.

"Status of the escape pod area, please, Mickey."

'I am afraid we have lost a number of pods, Boss. Pods 8, 9,10 and 11 have been destroyed.'

For several moments panic gripped me and my eyes closed in silent prayer. I resisted thoughts of defeat and I bowed my head in frustration. The faces of many crew members, plus a good deal of the Andromeda City folk flashed before my eyes—I may not see them again. The weight of leadership hung like a millstone around my neck. I thought of Carla—our escape pod, number one, should still be okay. Number ten, Gary Pearson's pod, however, among the obliterated number, released me from the need to deal with his treason problem. This thought bothered me and I decided it would have been better to have all those people alive, despite the problem with Pearson.

'We have scored a direct hit on the third warship, President Commander. It would appear their shields are not as strong as ours. There is still evidence of limited power but I think the vessel will be unable to continue in the fight.'

This brought some relief but the shadow craft still remained above us, unharmed. Our nukes, distracted by the enemy intercept-mechanisms, missed their intended target.

"Antimatter canons?"

'No change in status, Boss.'

"Is our compression-counter system able to continue operating?"

My concern for this particular system soared with sudden trepidation—without it the immense gravitational compression, under the Andromeda's extreme velocity, would crush us to pulp. This is an autonomous function, separate from all the other life-support provisions, designed to be the last casualty in a ship breakup. Even Mickey, by intent of the Andromeda's designers, exercised zero control over its operation. It functioned in conjunction with the propulsion system and kicked in with the steady increase of velocity.

'No concern there for the moment, President Commander—It would only stop operating when the vessel starts to disintegrate.'

"You make it sound like a distant possibility, Mickey but I'll take your word for it."

'Two nukes targeting shadow ship are on their away, Boss. Hold tight—I am taking evasive action.'

∞∞

Thirty-one

Enemy Missiles

The Andromeda corkscrewed through space, a maneuver I never knew it possessed. I wondered what the escape pod occupants experienced with their gravity status still intact. Carla, now without me would curse my pig-headedness in my decision, to remain on the bridge. Too late to change my mind—the route to the escape pod area had been cut off.

'Missiles incoming. Prepare for impact.'

"Why the fuck are our intercept flares so ineffective?"

'The present enemy is using something different to what the first Crustan attackers used, Boss. It appears to be a counter measure to a counter measure.'

Seconds reeled off the clock. When the missiles struck us the Andromeda pitched and yawed, shuddered and shook, until I thought we would disintegrate. The emergency lights failed and the bridge plunged into darkness.

'Our propulsion system has been severely compromised, President Commander. We can no

longer alter course or make any type of evasive maneuver.'

I now needed the EVA suit's twin spotlights to see—all the alarm icons failed and my mind prepared for the worst.

"Are you still with me, Mickey—report."

'Assessing damage, Boss. Our forward nuke bays have been damaged and the antimatter-cannons will still not prime. We are unfortunately defenseless. May I suggest you contact the overseer of the shadow vessel and talk. The Andromeda is a sitting duck.'

"They will board us, Mickey. I can't allow that to happen."

The alternative is not an option, President Commander.'

The escalation of our dire circumstances left us with no alternative but to do as the AI suggested.

I reached over to the translator device and steeled myself to make the call. It impacted on my sense of failure but no options remained other than the complete destruction of our ship. This thought did encroach for a brief while but I could not consider the destruction of the vessel while breath still remained in my body. I punched the translator's keypad and spoke:

"This is President Commander Conroy of the Andromeda. I am calling the overseer of the

Crustan vessel, presently situated above our ship. I am asking for your terms of surrender."

The emergency lights came back on and with it, a limited operation of the holo-receiver. My message must have gone through but silence reigned. I waited. A full minute passed before the holo-receiver put up a fuzzy hologram of a fierce-faced Crustan.

"Your message is acknowledged Human Commander Conroy. Prepare for a Crustan boarding party. We will be coming aboard with a heavily armed squad of enforcers. Any resistance will be aggressively put down. You will light up your main entrance hatch so we can make a tunnel connection. Do not be mistaken into thinking it will be possible for you destroy our ship while it is docked for boarding. Any such attempt will be detected and you will pay with your lives."

The Crustan's eyes flamed with anger but the voice steady and calm, a creature used to authority and instant obedience.

To light up the entrance under our present limited power might be a problem.

"Can we do that, Mickey?" I asked.

'There is an emergency light close to the hatch. I will activate it, President Commander.'

I let the overseer know there would be a light. He made a terse acknowledgement and the hologram went blank. I knew they would be curious as to the technology we employed and perhaps happy not to obliterate us until a party came aboard to establish more information. This could be to our advantage. It at least gave me a limited time to come up with some escape strategy.

"We might have about one hour before their party arrives on board. Is there anything we can do, Mickey?"

'I would have suggested you evacuate to your escape pod while they are boarding, Boss, but the corridor from the bridge to the pod area has been compromised by the emergency sealing doors. These cannot be opened until full power is restored—this unfortunately means you will not be able to escape from the bridge area so I cannot initiate the Andromeda's destruction.'

The AI would not be able to override its programmed protocol so it could not sacrifice me, no matter the purpose.

"I have an idea," I answered. "Evacuate the pods that are still serviceable. I will stay here until the boarding party enters the craft. There is an emergency hatch behind the main con wall that leads to the outside corridor where the remaining EEP's are situated. I can escape in one of those and by adding a little propulsion to the capsule, can hopefully catch up with the escape pods. You would not be placing me at any more risk than if I stayed and was taken prisoner by the Crustans."

The AI remained silent for a few moments.

'I can do that, Boss,' it said.

"The pod evacuation route can be from the roof area or the bottom of the vessel. If we chose to evacuate from the bottom of the vessel the Crustans would not know what was happening. They would pick up the escape pods leaving but being connected to us by an umbilical tunnel and with their squad of crabs busy boarding there will be nothing they can do in a hurry."

'It is a viable plan, President Commander. The escape pods will have a head start of millions of kilometers by the time the Crustans can get under way. There is also the crippled vessel to think of.'

"I will make my way to the hatch. The EEP's launch directly out the roof so I can't disguise my escape but I'll take my chances."

'Preparing to initiate escape of viable pods. When the Crustan party sets foot aboard the Andromeda the pods will be deployed. You can choose your moment, President Commander but I will not destroy the Andromeda until I know you are safely evacuated. It has been an honor to serve you, Sir.'

I felt an emotion with regards to Mickey's benediction. Our commune with one another encompassed many years and it seemed surreal to say goodbye. The AI's involved in my life always took on personalities which I deemed to be real people—as real as any of the human crew members—my interaction with them registered on a sentient level. There remained one last protocol to observe: to make a quick entry in the Commander's log. Even when a ship's future hangs in the balance it remains a commander's last responsibility.

Mickey would transfer the entry to all the escape pod computers so the record would be available for posterity.

Commander's log.
President Commander, Dr. Beckett Conroy.
18th June, 2367 CE.

The Andromeda has been severely damaged by alien enemy fire. The Crustans are a war-like species from another dimension and are invading our universe for life support supplies and minerals. We are adrift without power, protective shields are down and weapons will not prime. They will be boarding us soon. The remaining and undamaged escape pods, containing about half the ship's compliment, will launch the moment the enemy boards our vessel. The other half of our number have been killed by enemy fire. I will be the last to leave the ship by means of an EEP before the Master Control flight Computer, Mickey, destroys the Andromeda and hopefully, takes the alien craft with it.......

∞∞

Thirty-two

Enemy Boarding Party

With translator in hand and much trepidation in my heart a quick glance around the bridge for the last time brought pangs of sadness. I said goodbye to Mickey and floated in the zero G toward the emergency hatch in the wall behind the con. The EVA suit possessed enough oxygen to last me for about eight hours but once in the EEP, a connection to a breathable air generator and hibernation process, would give me several years of stasis. The pod's computer would direct the thrusters to home-in on Hera-Soter and wake me on arrival in the planet's orbit.

It would have been great to make contact with Carla's escape pod, to let her know my status, but this could not happen under the circumstances. Her heartbreak, at my apparent demise, saddened me but a positive attitude remained—we would be reconciled, be it in life or death—I believed this with all my heart.

The hatch opened with some difficulty, perhaps due to the irregular services performed by the maintenance bots. A quick peek into the corridor exposed a scene of chaos to my eyes. A maintenance service cabinet, broken loose from its anchors in the wall opposite the hatch, spewed all its contents into the zero G atmosphere. Service tools and clothes, vials of different colored lubricants, all floated around in silence. Further along the passageway the EEP station, meant for bridge patrons like myself, appeared intact and two of the pods displayed dim, green status lights. The third pod status light, above an empty birth-pad, glowed red.

I made my way to the station and keyed in a code to open the first EEP's canopy. This pod would become my home until I reached Hera-soter. The cockpit, with a narrow compression couch and no space for lateral movement, produced a claustrophobic atmosphere for its lone occupant. The integrated physio and hibernation equipment, to sustain my body in stasis for an extended period, took up most of the space and it felt like a coffin. A hose, for circulation of the green life-suspension liquid, clicked onto my EVA suit. The equipment would begin its magic after the computer launched the EEP. A small lever at my side brought the instruments to a ready status and the head's up display blinked into reality. I reached over to press the "close-canopy" key and waited. The cover did not budge. I pressed harder—still no movement.

An alarm-light blinked on the HUD to indicate a malfunction with the mechanism. It must have jammed, perhaps due to the enemy strike. The canopy wouldn't budge no matter how much pressure I placed on the key—I cursed the Crustans. I needed to unhitch my EVA from the support system and change pods. The problem of malfunction could be rectified but it would take too long.

I disconnected my EVA from the life-support system and clambered out of the pod hindered by the cumbersome EVA suit. Did I ever mention my sense of timing sucks? The Crustans chose the moment of my transfer to appear at the ship's outside entrance. The outside hatch opened and placed me in their line of sight—there would be no escape for me.

A Crustan, in a spacesuit of complex design, stood framed in the entrance and stared in my direction. It surprised me to see a bipedal creature, with two sets of arms, complimented by two long, spindle-like legs the species appeared larger than on the holo's initial view.

I froze in the corridor—the Crustan looked at my still form for an eternity before it moved forward, into the Andromeda's entrance portal. The rest of its squad floated along behind in the Zero G. I huddled against the open door of the EEP, an attempt to blend in with the pod-station. To add to my consternation a sudden vibration in the walls emanated from the pod station—the corridor bucked and heaved like a rodeo horse—then it dawned on me; the launch of the escape pods.

The Aliens, with looks of alarm, stopped to hold onto whatever wall-protrusions they could find, until the vibration ceased. Then the leader pointed a gloved talon at me and they came on with as much speed as the conditions would allow. I stood still and waited. My heart almost failed as two of the Crustans grabbed my arms, one on each side, to pin me against the wall. The leader gave some sort of signal and they held me there, each with a gloved hand, gripped on the EEP canopy, for balance. The leader moved off toward the sealed door, which led to the bridge and tried in vain to open it. The emergency hatch came under scrutiny. Left open by me to gain entrance into the corridor, it begged the alien's attention and he moved toward it. The total alien party comprised of the leader and four armed soldiers. My detainment occupied two of these, which left the remnants of the squad to follow their leader through the hatch to the bridge.

After a lengthy sojourn the leader and his two cohorts returned. I guessed they must have satisfied their curiosity with regards to the level of technology aboard the Andromeda. A small oblong box situated on one of the upper left arms sported a cable to the large helmet and I assumed whatever the Crustan saw would be videoed and stored for later scrutiny.

The overseer of the warship must have been in constant contact with the squad leader. I assumed they witnessed the departure of the escape pods and would have a question about the whereabouts of our vessel's crew. The squad leader floated off along the corridor, with one of the soldiers, toward the verticap station. If they intended to search the ship it would take a long time, given the size of Andromeda and they would find their way impeded by the emergency doors, which sealed off important areas of the ship. The two major hull breaches would have caused many adjacent areas to close down.

Good luck to you, you fucking crab, I thought. I looked toward the open exit hatch and noticed the umbilical tunnel for the Crustan crew's transition could no longer be seen. The warship overseer must have withdrawn it as a precaution against any treachery on my behalf. My mind screamed out for a solution to my dilemma. How would I escape my captor's clutches and where could I go? The deck seemed stacked against me. If it became possible to shake off the two Crustan goons, my sole solution would be to consult Mickey about a place to hide, away from the EEP station. The pod still remained my salvation in any bid for a possible escape from the Andromeda.

A sudden realization dawned on me. I should still have contact with Mickey through the radio comm of my EVA suit—our benediction earlier, seemed so final and any thought of further conversation seemed pointless. My continued presence on the ship would mean the destruction of the Andromeda could not proceed. I glanced down at the comm switch, situated on a keypad attached to my left arm and understood Mickey's silence. The comm switch rested in the off position.

I couldn't reach it with my two arms pinned against the EEP station door. The squad leader returned from his venture and motioned to catch my attention. He wanted to communicate with me but did not know if I possessed a translator. After a moment of consideration he fiddled around with the comm cords between my helmet and wrist-pad in an attempt to figure out how we could establish some communication. With the cord from my helmet disconnected and held in its hand, the leader scrutinized the connection for a moment. He must have worked out a method of transmission. After a brief consultation with one of the others an auxiliary cord appeared in one of the soldier's hands—when I say hands, the appendages appeared more like talons.

The leader grabbed the cord and stared at the connection which appeared to be the same size as the connection on my helmet. The fittings did not match but he knew how to overcome it. A tube of unknown substance appeared in his hand—from a toolkit attached to the front of the alien's suit—

and applied it to my helmet's radio connection. The cord ends stuck together and to my surprise we possessed a workable connection. With the other end of the cord inserted into his helmet he attempted to communicate with me.

Some gruff clicks and clucks emanated from the alien as he spoke and I shook my head, to indicate I could hear but not understand its words. The leader thought for a moment and then one of the soldiers made a suggestion. I could see the two huge eyes open wide in acknowledgement and he flicked a switch on the arm pad. A translator came into play—impressed I realized their technology, in certain areas, surpassed ours. Ozzy's translator hung on a protrusion inside the vacated EEP.

"You are the commander of this vessel?"

The voice sounded gruff but calm.

I steeled myself to answer. "Yes I am the human, President Commander Beckett Conroy of the Research vessel, Andromeda."

"You fired on the Galipon and destroyed it but the crew evacuated."

"I fired on them because they wanted to board my craft and I couldn't allow that."

"Where is the rest of your crew?"

"They have already left the vessel."

He stared at me with blood-red eyes in as-sessment of my answer. There appeared to be a moist atmosphere within the helmet and I remembered Ozzy's words; these creatures were amphibious.

"Escape pods?"

"Yes".

He contemplated the status quo for several seconds. "No matter—we will catch them up and take them prisoner."

"You don't say."

"We have a higher velocity capability than your Andromeda."

"So I noticed."

I realized every second these bastards could be delayed gave the escape pods more time to put a greater distance between the two positions. If the pods could reach Hera-soter before the Crustans caught up with them they may have a chance to mount a defense.

"Your ship is internally sealed off, why is that?"

"Your missile strikes must have breached our hull in some places."

"What has happened to the computer running the systems."

This crab did not appear to be stupid. I didn't want them to have access to Mickey so I lied.

"The Master Control Computer shut down with all the other systems—it is a measure designed to prevent all the ship's information being accessed by pirates like you."

"You call me a pirate but your species is in violation of the space-time in this area of the universe."

I didn't give a shit about what he thought—as long as I could distract him from any idea to commandeer Mickey.

"You are not even from this universe you Crustan bastard. Don't try to make out that you and your species belong here."

The squad leader inclined his huge helmeted head and stared at me. This information should not have slipped out. How would I explain a knowledge of their dimension?

"Enough talk. We need to get back to our ship—you will accompany us and when we have sucked out all your knowledge we will dispose of you."

"Nice of you to let me know your intensions—you can go fuck yourself."

The Crustan ignored my comment and touched the keypad on his one arm. He became occupied for a short spell and I assumed he made a call for the return of the umbilical tunnel. They all faced away from the entrance, focused on me and did not see what took place behind their backs. My eyes opened wide in astonishment as I peered past the aliens at the open exit hatch. A figure materialized as if out of some dream and stood there in silent observance of our group huddle. It came from outside the ship—or so I thought. In the moment I realized the figure wore an Andromeda EVA suit and this confused the hell out of me. Did someone stay behind after the pods left? Could this be a dream?

∞∞

Thirty-three

A Visitor

The Crustan soldiers turned, with me lodged between them, toward the exit. The sight of the suited figure at the exit hatch stopped them in their tracks. With weapons still loose at their sides they gaped and appeared confused. The leader turned to look beyond his soldiers and saw the object of their awe. He grabbed a short, stubby stick-like object, attached to his belt and pointed it in the general direction of the hatch. At the same moment I saw the umbilical tunnel, extended from the warship snap back into place over the exit, behind the mysterious spacer.

Like a bolt of lightning, a bluish-red light shot out from the mysterious astronaut's helmet and enveloped the squad of five Crustans— for an instant a sharp pain shot through my forehead and the aliens collapsed onto the floor. Apart from occasional jerk of limbs they appeared to have been neutralized. I looked with some confusion at the scene. Why am I still conscious and upright? The spacer in the EVA glided along the corridor toward me and stopped to observe the prone aliens. With a single motion of a gloved hand he lifted his helmet visor. I gasped. It couldn't be—Lieutenant Sparkle.

The only words I could muster in my wonderment, "How in the f—".

The Lieutenant's suit showed signs of severe abuse by the outside elements.

'Greetings, President Commander.'

"You managed to escape the explosion. How in God's name did you do that?"

'We can discuss my fortunate escape later, President Commander. Right at this moment there is another squad floating along that umbilical tunnel and if we stay here they will destroy us. I don't think they know about me yet—so let's get going.'

"What's your plan, assuming you have one, Sparkle?'

'I managed to make contact with Mickey and asked for a route, using emergency tunnels, to the antimatter magazine.'

"We are out of luck with those weapons, I'm afraid. They won't prime."

'I know why, President Commander. Mickey eventually worked it out too but by then it was too late to do anything—you had already been taken prisoner by the Crustans. All it will take to initiate priming is a physical adjustment to the perimeter-rods so that the firing mechanisms can activate.'

"Are you proposing an antimatter strike at their craft?"

'The position of the antimatter canons is fortuitous. The one on the port side is presently in a perfect position, pointing directly at the enemy warship alongside us.'

"But won't there be a tremendous explosion, taking the Andromeda with it?"

'The antimatter projectiles do not explode on contact. Immediately after impact, antimatter spreads like a cancer, annihilating the ship's hull in miniaturized and accelerated reactions. Although there'll be a sudden expansion of space between the two craft, the Andromeda will survive it.'

"What about the umbilical tunnel? It's connected to the Andromeda. Won't the chain reaction continue through the tunnel?"

'The expansion of space will take care of that. The Andromeda will be violently pushed away from the Crustan craft and the tunnel's connection will be severed.'

Sparkle seemed to have thought this whole scenario through to its end. I hoped his calculations proved correct. We pushed ourselves back along the corridor toward the verticap station. Next to the elevator's entrance and situated in the wall, an emergency hatch concealed a spiral stairway which wound its way to the roof area. The maintenance bots used it in the course of weapon's systems service.

Sparkle led the way. He knew where we needed to go. Once in the maze of short corridors and stairwells we scurried along like rabbits in a warren. After a few minutes a hatch marked "Antimatter Canon Magazine" came into view and Sparkle touched the keypad to give us access. We both squeezed through the narrow entrance and I gained my first view of the priming mechanisms.

'This won't take me long, President Commander. Would you please focus this light onto the inner workings of the mechanisms?' He unclipped a slim-line flashlight from his upper arm and handed it to me. After the removal of a panel cover the android bent over and peered into the cavity behind. I did my best to focus the light onto the areas where it placed its hands.

'I have the perimeter rods—the adjustments are extremely subtle.'

Sparkle continued to work on the rods without further comment. I wondered about the arrival of the second Crustan party in the main corridor.

"How did you neutralize that Crustan squad?" I asked.

Sparkle continued his adjustments. *'The Crustans, if you remember President Commander, are amphibious and prefer an atmosphere that is heavily moist. Their suit-systems are de-*

signed to create this desired hydro-mixture which they find easier to breath than our air. All I did was superheat the moisture in their helmets with my eye-lasers. This caused a temporary boiling sensation, stunning them.'

"I felt a sharp pain but beyond that it didn't affect me."

'Your human blood is much thicker than the moisture and it wasn't enough to take you down, President Commander.'

"What's the plan once you have the perimeter rods properly adjusted?"

'I'm banking on the Crustan Commander not taking fright at our escape and being greedy enough to want to find out more about the Andromeda. Hopefully he will keep his troops on board to search for us. Once these rods are adjusted I will begin the priming. Fortunately the magazine has its own source of power.'

"Solar Batteries—I remember seeing this on the design specs Ozzy gave us. How long will the priming take?"

'If all goes well, about five seconds.'

"Do we remain in here when the fun takes place?"

'It should be safe enough for you, President Commander.'

"I hope you are right about the effect of the antimatter reactions. We are pretty close to them. What about the other ship?"

'The other ship appears to be severely damaged. I think they are hoping this one will rescue them once the Andromeda has been dealt with.'

"They have a nasty surprise waiting for them," I said.

The android straightened without warning—the flashlight flew from my hand and floated off to one side as he peered toward the door. I knew some vibration beyond my senses must have caught its attention. Androids possess built-in sensing equipment to warn them of dangers that could lurk behind walls, doors or in hidden, confined spaces.

"What is it, Sparkle?"

'It must be the second party of aliens, President Commander. They must be able to track our heat signature residue through the corridors. They are getting close to our position. I must complete the adjustments'

Sparkle dove back into the cavity, extending his bionic hands to reach the rods again. I retrieved the flashlight and focused it down onto the work area again. With my heart in my mouth I kept my eyes riveted on the magazine entrance hatch.

"Are you nearly done?" My nerves were beginning to buckle.

'Nearly done, Sir. Just a few more turns of the rod's micro-spindle and then a quick check on the projectile loading conveyor.'

I did not understand the meaning behind the statement but it didn't matter—he knew what to do.

"How close are the boarding party to the magazine?" I asked.

'Close. If the door opens throw yourself to the left and try to get behind the loading hoist, President Commander. I will be firing both my lasers and you do not want get in the way of the beams.'

"I hear you—to the left it will be."

Sparkle worked on the adjustment while I kept my eyes riveted on the hatch—the adjustment appeared complex. If the Crustans interrupted us, would we be able to get the cannons primed in time before the Warship's overseer took action? My guess—he would blast us all out of space-time if he knew of our present position. It would take a few seconds for the squad leader to guess our intensions and report the matter to his boss. I doubted if the Overseer would hesitate to sacrifice his soldiers to save his ship. We would be obliterated.

Eternity passed by and the adjustments continued.

I became anxious. "For fuck sake, Lieutenant—is the job not finished yet?"

'Patience, Sir. This is a delicate job." Another couple of seconds passed before he jerked back into an upright position. 'There, it's done—the rods are calibrated and the conveyor is working fine. Priming has started.'

As it turned out the lieutenant's statement brought but a brief second of relief—the hatch flew open and a Crustan soldier with his two huge, red eyes ablaze in concentration, stared at us.

Without hesitation I launched myself toward the projectile-conveyor hoist as Sparkle's eyes lit up a brilliant red, to emit lasers in the direction of the enemy. I didn't wait to see the result but pulled myself behind the corner of the conveyor and burrowed into the corner of the magazine, as far in as possible. The room filled with smoke and an unfamiliar mist. The Crustan soldier fired his weapon at the same time Sparkle's lasers hit their target. I cringed in my hole and hoped to God the lieutenant survive the Crustan's onslaught. I still needed to hear his full story. If the Crustan managed to destroy him I would never know how he came back to the Andromeda. Black smoke now billowed from the hatchway as I peeked around the corner of the hoist to see the red flash of the laser beam, like a welder's blow torch, continue its devastation.

After interminable seconds the entire magazine lurched and bucked, like a wild rodeo bull, my body turned a somersault and propelled me back into the room.

"Sparkle?" I shouted. "Are you okay?"

The comm remained silent and the thick smoke obscured my vision. The Andromeda yawed as if in the grip of some giant beast and I blacked out.

*

A voice called me from a great distance. The words unintelligible at first, like empty cans rolling around in a wooden container, became clearer. I opened my eyes to look into Sparkle's blue orbs. I recognized the confines of the magazine, now absent of the black smoke. I must have passed out.

"What happened?" I asked.

'I managed to activate the canon. The warship is no more and two of the Crustan boarding party are dead. There are more and must still be somewhere aboard our ship. We'll have to neutralize them before trying to restore systems on the Andromeda.'

"Do you think we'll be able to get things going again?"

'I have received a full damage report from Mickey and I am confident we will be able to restore gravity and lights. The hull breaches are sealed off but it will be some time before the bots are able to weld everything together. The propul-

sion system is not fixable and we will have to be inventive in order to guide the Andromeda back onto course.'

"Are we far off course?"

'By trillions of kilometers, President Commander.'

∞∞

Thirty-four

Tracking down the Enemy

Trillions of kilometers suggested an acute angle in trajectory and a great deal of space-time we would need to cover by means of a direction change—but without the propulsion system we as good as dead in the water. The Andromeda still maintained the initial impetus of 75 percent C but course changes required propulsion, generated by special thrusters. We would have to devise a workable plan. The Crustan soldiers, still loose somewhere in the ship, would not be difficult to find—Mickey and Sparkle's sensing abilities made a quick discovery of the heat residues left behind in the wake of their escape. I needed to get back to the Bridge.

"Is the ship's comm system still up and running?"

'It is working, President Commander, but you will need to switch to the emergency frequency.'

It now dawned on me why I could not contact Mickey. The normal frequency operated in conjunction with the main power source and the emergency frequency worked on solar batteries and retained a separate, closed system, which operated when the main power supply failed.

It took only a second to key in the instruction on the wrist-pad and after a few seconds of static, the clear and articulate voice of the Master Flight Computer caressed my ears.

'Welcome back, President Commander. I see Lieutenant Sparkle found you at last.'

"I have never been happier to meet up with an android, Mickey. If it were not for Sparkle we would be prisoners of the Crustans."

'Indeed, President Commander. His timing was brilliant.'

"We need to find the rest of the Crustan boarding party. Do you have a fix on any of them yet?" I asked.

'I detect heat residue in the warehouse area —there are two bodies moving along in a corridor leading to the uranium stockpile.'

"Good work. Are we in any danger if they discover the stockpile?"

'If they understand the technology—which we should assume they do—the uranium could be used to make an explosive device. They would need to get into the propulsion area and try to use one of the reactors.'

"Shit—that could have serious repercussions for all of us." I said.

'Could we try to approach them and strike some sort of a bargain?' Sparkle asked.

"What could we offer them?"

'Their lives and a possible transfer to their crippled ship,' Sparkle answered.

"It's not a bad idea, Lieutenant but I think we would have difficulty in getting them to trust us —we have just blown their mothership into oblivion."

'I think it's worth a try, President Commander.'

I considered the option. We could use Ozzy's translator; it still hung on a protrusion in the EEP. The more I thought about the plan the more it appealed to me.

"Let's give it a try. Mickey—work out a quick route from the main corridor to the warehouse area. I assume the power will still be off for a while?"

'Correct, President Commander. I have only just managed to communicate with some of the maintenance bots again. Many of them are out of commission. I will send the Lieutenant a schematic of the viable passages and stairwells.'

Sparkle and I climbed through the scorched magazine hatch and moved back toward the main deck. At least we knew the Crustan's present position and needed not worry about being ambushed. I prayed Mickey would be able to establish full power again so we could restore gravity back to our vessel.

The other crippled warship, required consideration. If they still possessed any operational weapons we might be in trouble but so far, we detected zero movement. If able, they would have fired on us in the aftermath of the third ship's destruction. Ozzy's intel referred to three Crustan ships with a military capability. Three exploration craft still remained but, as deduced from the detection of the first Crustan vessel, possessed no military capabilities.

"Mickey—do you have anything on the crippled warship? Is there any sign of life aboard?"

'My heat signature sweep shows no sign of life, President Commander.'

"Is it possible they have escaped in pods?"

'It is possible, Boss. The nuclear cloud of excess radiation would have rendered the release of pods incapable of detection.'

"We can't offer our prisoners any hope of joining them then."

'We could still offer them a ride to Herasoter and an attempt to contact one of their exploration vessels,' said Sparkle.

"I guess you're right, Lieutenant."

We continued on our way through the maze of corridors and stairwells. After fifteen minutes we arrived at the final hatch, which led to the main corridor and made our way through to the EEP station, to retrieve the translator. The five neutralized Crustan's from the initial boarding party must have revived and moved off into the umbilical tunnel before the warship's destruction, in need of first aid. They might have been in the tunnel when the two ships separated. I decided a laser-rifle would be an advantage if our negotiations with the Crustans failed and secured a weapon from one of the emergency pods. Each EEP contained one rifle with a limited charge.

"How much charge do you still have for your continued operation, Sparkle?"

'It is down to five percent, President Commander but there is no time to waste. I will have to get by on what I have.'

"I have the laser-rifle—all you have to do is lead us through the maze. Do you know the way?"

The lieutenant acknowledged receipt of Mickey's schematic and we moved off on the arduous trek through the myriad of emergency corridors, this time to the warehouse area. It took a full half-hour to reach the warehouse level. Sparkle's heat-residue beams took over from Mickey's heat-signature sensors and detected the Crustan's presence to be two bays over, from our position. The android, in an attempt to conserve energy talked little and used a slower, longer stride. The confrontation with the enemy would be in my hands. Sparkle would not have the power left to operate his lasers if we got into trouble. I realized I did not have the cable-connection for direct communication with the Crustans. The translator would not be able to work due to the lack of power—no atmosphere existed within the ship. No air, meant no sound. I relayed my concern to the android. To conserve energy the lieutenant kept the answer to a minimum.

'You may have to use signs to indicate we are taking them prisoner.'

Without the means of a verbal communication the odds stacked themselves against a peaceful solution. If they submitted to incarceration in the brig we might have time to resolve the power crisis to allow an audible, verbal conversation.

We drew close to their position. It appeared to be in a smaller storage bay next to the uranium rod storage. An emergency hatch stood open between the two bays and I could see a compromised door-lock mechanism. Whatever weapon the Crustan soldiers used, it contained a mean potency. My thoughts drifted to the strange mist-residue I saw in the antimatter magazine while under attack—it might be the emission from a particle accelerator.

I needed to be cautious in my approach. They may even be privy to our presence. Sparkle indicated the Crustans to be on the move and would pass by the spot where we waited. We hid behind a stack of crates which contained propulsion spares and I kept an eye on the corridor. The two Crustans floated into view, with four UR rods between them. They did not seem to suspect our presence and Mickey's deduction, as to their intentions, appeared to be correct—the soldier in front scrutinized the HUD on the inside of its visor. The faint picture I could see in reverse appeared to be an infrared schematic of what lay ahead of them. They must have understood the ship's propulsion came from a set of reactors, hence their possession of the four UR rods. This brought some enlightenment with regards to the advanced technology at their disposal. Given the opportunity their efforts could lead to the Andromeda's destruction.

I stepped out into the corridor to confront them. My one hand held onto the corner crate for support while the other gripped the laser. Sparkle stepped out with me to provide an extra deterrent—they would remember the lasers. We hovered in front of them and tried to keep the laser as steady as possible. The two soldiers stopped their forward drift and stared at me. My rifle pointed at the lead Crustan's helmet and I indicated with my free hand for them to sit down. They released the UR rods which floated away, along the corridor .

The two aliens made no further movement. I could see short stick-like weapons attached to their sides and hoped they would not attempt to shoot it out. Sparkle moved out from behind me into full view and I could see the fear register in the lead Crustan's eyes. With swift movements both soldiers snapped up weapons to fire but before the muzzles levelled out to cut us down I fired the laser-rifle. The resultant blast flattened the two aliens against the wall, and ripped their suits open. This caused an explosion of alien innards and blood, brought on by the pressure differential, which floated outwards in all directions.

I turned to Sparkle for a reaction but he made gave no acknowledgement. His store of energy at its lowest possible level, required an urgent recharge. A charge station could be found in every major corridor of the ship so I grabbed his hand and set off. The charging stations all possessed an emergency supply, compliments of the solar trans-former energy supply to the waste disposal and emergency comm systems.

∞∞

Thirty-five

Quick-fix propulsion System

"Is any headway being made by the maintenance bots, Mickey?"

With the lieutenant plugged into a charge
station on one of the lower-deck corridors I made
my way via the emergency route to the bridge. The
immediate priorities lay in the restoration of the
ship's power and gravity, plus the need to work out
a way to make a direction change. Every minute
that passed took the Andromeda millions of kilometers out of its way, with more time added to the
duration of our journey. A new hope gripped my
prognosis for the future—a real change of circumstance from the scenario that confronted me an
hour ago. A sense of euphoria filtered through my
trauma-logged mind and in addition, a new lease
on life.

I thought of Carla and the crew members.
By now they would be in hibernation, aboard their
escape pods, in silent transition to our new home
planet, oblivious of our vessel's narrow escape
from destruction. Unlike the Andromeda, the escape pods could handle entry into an atmosphere
and would be able to land safely under the guid-

ance of their flight computers. The occupant's resuscitation system would kick in to restore all onboard, back to consciousness. The Andromeda, however, designed for orbit and not to land on any type of flat terrain, made the escape pods necessary for transfer to the planet's surface. By my rough calculation at least eighteen months still remained to the completion of our journey.

"How are the repair bots doing, Mickey?"

'There are only two maintenance bots available to work on restoring power and gravity, President Commander. With four hull breaches in different places, the remaining operational bots are struggling to cope.'

"Any idea how long it's going to take?"

'I would say another two hours, Boss.'

"Power is the most important aspect of providing a new directional guidance system for the ship. We'll be adding months, perhaps years onto our journey if we don't work something out quickly."

'I have a possible solution to the guidance system, Boss. It is based on a paper written by a junior propulsion tech working on solutions to emergency scenarios, before the Andromeda was launched.'

"Tell me about it—I'm ready to consider any measure within our ability make the necessary changes."

'The external thruster-rockets are not damaged but the supply of energy to them has been destroyed beyond a quick-fix. It would take months to restore the power supply in the normal way. We require a long, heavy-duty power cable to be stripped from another part of the life-support system and laid through a disposal portal to fabricated, distribution boxes which would be welded on to the hull, close to each of the four main thruster rockets.'

"—and a connection could then be made to the auxiliary solar-powered transformer that runs the waste disposal system. How long to do this, Mickey?"

'About two hours, Boss.'

"Two hours to restore the normal power and gravity—and two hours to make up this emergency system? I think we leave the power and gravity to concentrate on the thrusters. It's more important we get the Andromeda pointed in the right direction."

I will redirect the two available bots with the relevant instructions, President Commander.

My EVA reminded me of a limited oxygen level for the fourth time. The normal oxygen replenishment of suits took place from a nozzle protrusion, situated next to the EVA cabinet. Due to the lack of direct power it would be necessary to go back to the storage area on the lower level where the bodies of the two dead Crustan soldiers still lay in the main warehouse passageway—should have thought of this before the arduous journey to the bridge.

Oxygen cylinders stacked in one of the bays could be connected to the EVA and the oxygen life-support tank replenished. Without further self-retribution, the trek back through the emergency hatch and consequent corridors, got underway—at least I knew the route now.

The station where Sparkle still languished for recharge purposes provided a brief rest period for me. I couldn't relax for too long as my suit's computer kept up its limited-oxygen tirade and wore more on me than the physical effort to guide my trajectory through hatches and corridors. The lieutenant seemed to be fine. He managed a grin, with the synthetic skin at the corners of his mouth scrunched up and a raised bionic hand, to greet me. The charge level registered at thirty-five per-cent.

"Heading down to the oxygen storage bay, Lieutenant—should be back within half-an-hour or so."

The android acknowledged my gesture. I pushed on through another emergency hatch and down a spiral flight of stairs to the next level. Once in the warehouse corridor I kicked off in the direction of the two Crustans, still crumpled up against the blood-splattered wall. The strange color of their blood struck me as odd. It possessed a very dark, purplish hue in the dull luminescence of the emergency lights. This might have to do with the hydro-moist atmosphere they breathed. I noticed something different. The one body now lay against the adjacent wall. A slew of blood indicated the original position from whence the creature dragged itself. Propped up against the wall with the large, helmeted head twisted around facing me, I thought it may still be alive. In careful inspection of the weapon, still clutched in the alien's hand, I tried to release it from the death grip. This action landed me in a great deal of trouble.

A beam of supercharged particles shot out of the muzzle and hit me on the shoulder. The power of the blast knocked my body backwards. Pain exploded along the length of my arm and paralyzed it while I turned a cartwheel to float back, down the corridor. My senses faded along with the ability to think and darkness descended on my surroundings. The suit computer changed its calm repeat of low oxygen level to an urgent, *'oxygen level critical'* as the EVA vented the last dregs of precious life-support into my helmet.

∞∞

Thirty-six

Getting back on Course

The noise seemed far away at first but with a sudden rush sound returned through the helmet speakers to my eardrums and with it returned the reality of my predicament. The vivid dream about Carla disappeared in a flash and left the dullness of the emergency lights to illuminate the corridor. A head materialized and eyes stared at me—Sparkle.

'Don't try to move, President Commander— relax, until your strength returns.'

My foggy brain made a gradual return to reality. "Where the fuck did you come from, Lieutenant?"

'My sensors picked up the release of particles from the alien's weapon and I knew you were in trouble.'

"I can't seem to stay out of it, can I?"

'The Crustan's talon remained hooked to the trigger-mechanism and I guess you must have touched the weapon?'

"Was it dead?"

'Indeed, Sir. The smallest movement would have set it off. Your Eva's auto-seal took over and plugged the tear in the fabric. I found you, uncon-

scious and floating, with no oxygen left in the suit's supply tank.'

I glanced at the cylinder ensconced in Sparkle's arm. A service-tube coupled to the back of my EVA provided the oxygen for my continued existence.

"Once again, I have you to thank for saving me, Sparkle."

'Always available to be of help, Sir.'

"You reminded me of my valet, Happydoo— he would always say he was happy to do anything for me."

Sparkle grinned synthetically. 'Androids cannot circumvent their programming, President Commander.'

"I assume you weren't able to receive a full charge because of me."

'Sixty-five percent will do for the time-being, Sir. We have important things to do.'

I maneuvered into an upright position but the sudden rush of blood to my head provoked a severe giddiness and it took some time to clear. With one hand on the lieutenant's shoulder I floated alongside him to the emergency hatch which led back toward the upper-deck. My head throbbed from the result of oxygen starvation but I considered myself lucky—but for Sparkle, I would not have survived. Fifteen minutes later we arrived at the bridge.

"How's the reconstruction work going, Mickey?"

The two maintenance bots are working well together, Boss. They stripped an HD cable from a process in the Andromeda City area and have laid it through a port to the outside of the hull. Four distribution boxes from other non-essential systems have been commandeered and the bots are connecting these to the rocket thrusters. A connection is yet to be made to the waste-disposal solar transformer.'

"How much longer?"

'One hour, Boss.'

"How far are we off course?"

'Thrust vector angle—22 degrees off our present trajectory and will require a twenty-four second burst to bring the Andromeda on course for Hera-soter, Boss.'

"Estimated arrival date in contrast to the escape pods?"

'We will arrive in orbit on the 12th of January 2369 CE, President Commander. The escape pods will precede us by two months and two days.'

"Is there any way we can let the pod computers know what has happened to the Andromeda?"

'The message has already been relayed but the occupants of the pods are all in hibernation

and will be for the rest of their journey. They are now four light-hours ahead of us, Boss.'

"So, the messages we send will reach the pod's computers before they arrive at Hera-soter?"

'Barring any unforeseen problems—yes, Boss.'

My relief could not be contained—I smashed a gloved fist into my open hand and shouted a loud, YES. Carla would know about our survival and could look forward to our reunion.

I felt a tiredness creep through my body and a sudden need for food and sleep.

"I am going to rest in the compression couch for a while. Sparkle, would you be so kind as to retrieve some concentrate from the canteen pantry?—I am famished."

'I will see what I can find for you, Sir.' The android turned and left via the emergency hatch.

The compression couch brought a welcomed respite for me and I strapped myself in, thinking I would wait for Sparkle to return, but the land of nod overtook me.

*

After a short sleep I awoke to find a bottle of water attached with a strap, to the couch. It floated above my head in the zero G. The suit's emergency liquid intake mechanism operated with flawless effectiveness after I attached the water-bottle to the clamp provided on the outside of the helmet.

On the inside of the helmet, below the visor, a special tube became activated as the water entered the suit via a membrane. The tube swiveled around inside the helmet to place its open end onto my bottom lip. The water tasted good despite the years of refrigeration. I managed to digest all of it and felt my body react to the timeous hydration. I looked around for the lieutenant but did not see him.

'If you are looking for Lieutenant Sparkle, he decided to check out the repair jobs,' said Mickey.

"I will join him—I need to see these areas for myself."

Ten minutes later, I joined Sparkle to check out the reconstruction of the thrusters. The final connection had been made to the waste-disposal's solar power system. The lieutenant communicated with the bots involved and they confirmed the system ready to go.

"System is a go, Mickey."

'Please return to the bridge, President Commander. The transition to thruster power can only be accomplished when you and the lieutenant are strapped into your respective safety couches.'

Sparkle and I ascended back to the bridge and made ready for the direction change. I prayed the reparations would be successful. If it did not work much time would be lost and we might even be hooped.

'Initiating direction change on count of three.'

I waited in trepidation. The surge of power to the thrusters caused a vibration to run through the entire ship's hull. Our improvised repairs would subject the finely tuned balance of weight on the outside of the craft to change and we could not be sure of the reaction. I felt no sensation of direction change take place but Mickey's voice soon dispelled my fears.

'Direction change effected. We are now on our way to Hera-soter.'

I breathed an immense sigh of relief. The blue light in Sparkle's eyes blinked several times and the synthetic grin creased his android features.

∞∞

Thirty-seven

Excerpt from the Andromeda Log.

*President Commander, Dr. Beckett Conroy.
12th January, 2369 CE.*

The journey has been long. We left Earth in January, 2324 CE and today, forty-five years later, I have the first visual of our new home. It is stunning; beautiful and beyond words to accurately describe—I must pinch myself every time I look at it—I could be looking at the Earth.....

"Behold the planet, Sparkle."

'It meets every life-support specification within tolerance limits, Sir. I am sure everyone will be very happy here.'

The long list of life-support parameters for humans, compiled by the Earth Relocation Project's Exo-planet Compatibility section, found harmonious agreement for all its requirements, bar a few. Gravity constraints were not quite what we are used to but given a little adjustment over time, humans will eventually come to see it as normal.

My heart's delight, to see my beautiful wife again, knew no bounds. The pleasure of a face to face brought a great sense of the odds we have all overcome. Eighteen months ago, when Sparkle and I struggled for our lives we held onto a small hope of survival but now we stood on the brink of our ultimate achievement.

The final piece of our puzzle came together when an epiphany came upon me—I remembered the device Ozzy gave me prior to the final show-down with the Crustans. I solicited the alien's help after our change in direction to the home-planet. On his arrival back aboard the Andromeda, Ozzy's reaction of joy at our victory overwhelmed me. He wrapped the multi-arms around my shoulders, bobbed, shuddered and farted air for several minutes. He confessed to the rigidity of his superiors, who refused to release him due to certain problems in the Lumbrian dimension— he tried to get them to spare a force of warships for our rescue but they deemed our loss not be a critical issue. He broke away, however, from a critical engagement when the emergency transmitter, in my possession, sent out the alarm.

After several days Ozzy left. Mickey gave him the precise time of our arrival in orbit around Hera-soter and he promised to return on my next signal. In order to conserve resources aboard the Andromeda I made a decision to go into hibernation for the final leg of the journey. The restoration of full Power and gravity made this possible—I said goodbye to Mickey and the Lieutenant, to be swallowed up by the green liquid for the remainder of the journey. A week before the Andromeda entered orbit, Mickey brought me back to consciousness. My first view on the holo-receiver, of Hera-soter cannot be explained with words.

The hues of blue and green, darker than the Earth's; the large cumulus type clouds and the untouched pristine vegetation, made it appear as a picture of unspoiled beauty I will never forget. The deep, dark-blue seas captivated my sense of wonder. I could only imagine what types of creatures called this beautiful paradise their home.

'Preparing to fire thrusters—final re-direction for Orbit.'

We needed to orbit the planet for several days before a trip to the surface could be undertaken. I couldn't wait to set foot on real soil again. Mickey gave me a long list of all the people who perished in the enemy strike. Five hundred and thirty-eight of the finest people, still entombed in the derelict pods would be released into space—their journey would one day end in the corona of some star. I asked Mickey to find some special words, to help me perform a ceremony while the others on Hera-soter could follow on the pod holo-receivers.

Since my resuscitation, video contact with Carla and the people happened every day. She looked more beautiful and radiant than ever, with a lovely, multicolored flower in her hair and a tight-fit, emergency pod survival coverall.

Mickey reset the Andromeda's systems to operate on the Hera-soter, dynamical cycle and which would require a huge adjustment for me. The planet rotated once every twenty hours, and provided ten hours of sunlight and the same for nights. Life took on a new lease as I prepared for orbit entry. Once the orbit proved stable I contacted Ozzy via the Distress Transmitter and waited for him to join us.

The compression couch-straps felt loose on me—weight must have been lost during the time of the enemy strikes and consequent escape of the Andromeda's demise.

'T-10 to firing of thrusters, prepare for short burn of fifteen seconds, President Commander.'

"Ready when you are, Mickey."

I looked over at Sparkle who stood, locked into the charging station behind the con. He gave me one of those synthetic smiles I could never interpret.

The short burn slowed the Andromeda's velocity and tilted the bow toward the planet and within a few moments the pull of gravity on the craft became evident. Hera-soter grew large on the holo-receiver—I could not take my eyes off it. I became conscious of the planet's sudden rapid rotation beneath us, compliments of the screen above my head. The green of vegetation and blue of water merged in a blur. A short while later the rotation slowed until the Andromeda reached optimum orbit velocity and the surface of the planet once again resolved into separate entities. Below us drifted the atmosphere, a deep, dark blue, lined with crimson and orange clouds. The star, Pegasi 51 shone its gorgeous, golden rays of mega-photons across the breadth of the scene to light up elements in the oxygen-rich air mixture and make them shine with an incandescent glow.   I doubt whether anything, other than Carla's beauty, could transcend the absolute state of awe I felt.

'Orbit velocity achieved—gravity stable, air-pressure stable and all other support systems are stable'

I reached beneath the loose flap of my coveralls to extract the distress device—time to make contact with my alien friend. I twisted the central control and a sudden glow emanated from within its glassy front.   A vibration, faint but distinct flowed into my hand as I held it close to my face.

I de-strapped from the compression couch and beckoned to Sparkle. We walked over to the forward viewing port and gazed with wonderment and intrigue at our new home. Mickey set all systems to automatic and prepared for transfer of oversight to the auto-pilot computer, which would keep the systems stabilized and in good order.

Sparkle and I would squeeze into the Orbitron with Ozzy and leave the Andromeda. I couldn't wait to see Carla's ecstatic face—there would be a tearful scene as we reunited with one another.

Two hours later, while I busied myself on the gym's treadmill under surveillance of Sparkle, Mickey purred through the comm.

'President Commander to the bridge.'

Sparkle gave me one of those grins.

"You never told me how you got back to the Andromeda after the explosion of the first Crustan Warship and after all that elapsed time," I said.

He repeated the grin and made it obvious he enjoyed the nurture of my curiosity.

'I will—one day when we are safely on Hera-soter, but for now let's say providence smiled on me.'

This expression made me laugh out aloud. "What would an android know about providence?"

'Enough to know that something happened beyond my sphere of influence.'

We walked to the verticap and stepped out onto the bridge.

"You called for me, Mickey?"

'Ossimantus has arrived—the Orbitron is in its usual place.

"Can you bring him to the bridge, Sparkle—post haste?

'With pleasure, President Commander.'

My final action as President Commander of the Andromeda arrived with a sense of mission accomplished as I prepared to remove the steel-canister with Mickey's processor, from its slot in the main-frame room. The AI would be reinstalled in one of the escape pods on Hera-soter's surface.

"Is your download complete, Mickey?"

'It is done President Commander. I am testing out the automatic flight system as we speak.'

'Hera-soter here we come,' said Sparkle.

∞∞

Thirty- eight

The Beautiful Planet

A joyful reunion followed Ozzy's return to the Andromeda. My old pal confessed he thought he might never see Carla or I again. He snuffed and expelled some air to make himself more comfortable.

"There are times I hate the Lumbrian seed-realm philosophy. We're not really allowed to help out the local inhabitants but I decided the time to break with protocol could not have been better—I see some things differently to the way my superiors see them, when it comes to the Crustan's involvement in one of our realms."

"I understand your predicament. As a child I watched videos of the last wild-game parks on Earth and could not get over how often endangered animals were left in their predicaments. I was told not to judge the overseers of the conservation programs. They felt nature provided its own way of balancing the odds," I said.

"Are you ready dear boy?—to be reunited with your loved one and the surviving crew?"

"I have never been more ready, my alien friend."

"Shall we depart?"

Sparkle and I led the way back to the Orbitron. This would be my first experience of travel in this unique way. We would not need to jump into another dimension but the ride to Hera-soter's surface would, without doubt, be a new encounter.

Ozzy entered the machine first and took up a position in the furthermost confines from the entrance. Sparkle and I, carried the steel canister between us and entered in behind him to find a space against the adjacent walls, opposite each other. The Lieutenant sported his cheeky grin as he eyed my discomfort in the cramped, position—a semi-crouch with arms stretched to the floor, and my hands in support of the upper body.

Ozzy touched some keys on a pad close to his head and a noise emanated from beneath us. A green glow engulfed the inside of the Orbiron as the noise escalated to high pitch and I felt a sudden sensation of movement. The trip lasted for about twelve minutes.

"We have arrived," said Ozzy.

Emotion overwhelmed me as the tears flowed down my cheeks. The entrance hatch opened and sunlight filtered through into the innards of the Orbitron. The wonderment of it all almost paralyzed my legs and I hesitated.

"Come on dear boy, come on—don't keep her waiting," Ozzy complained.

With a sudden surge of joy I flung myself out of the entrance and landed for the first time in forty-eight years, on real soil. A group of people, most of whom I recognized, gathered around me with long stares, smiles and laughter. I looked around for one face before I could acknowledge anyone but the sunlight blinded my vision and caused me to place my hands over my eyes. When I removed them she stood before me in silent appraisal. Tears streamed down her cheeks and the beautiful emerald, green eyes flashed in the sunlight. I stood with wobbly knees and stretched out my arms to her—she fell into my embrace—we stood there for a long time as those around us softly acknowledged their appreciation of our reunion.

"Welcome home, President Commander—I've waited over twenty months to see you again hon," said Carla.

I laughed and hugged her as tight as I could, with care not to break any bones.

"I have missed you so much, Sweetheart—I thought I might never see you again but thanks to the lieutenant and Ozzy, this day is a reality."

I turned to Sparkle and said, "Now, you can tell us how you managed to escape that explosion."

The cheeky grin returned. 'In good time, Sir —in good time.'

I felt a tap on my shoulder and turned to see Happydoo, a huge grin on his face, with his arms wide open—Carla must have taught him how to hug someone.

"What nonsense have you been up to, you bucket of bolts and rivets?"

Much to my joy, the foot-stomp routine followed before I hugged him.

Breaking from the android's clutches I grabbed Carla again and looked into her eyes.

"How do you like your new home, Sweetheart?"

"It's absolutely wonderful but it's not all good. We need to get you settled and then we'll talk."

Ozzy took his turn to greet Carla and for the first time I saw a tear in the large eye.

"Greetings my dear—I am so relieved to see the two of you back together again."

She embraced him for a long period of time. "Thank you for all you've done; to provide us with your knowledge and help. We couldn't have pulled this mission off without you," she said.

Happydoo pointed to a path. *'We need to get back to Pod Village.'*

Carla grabbed my arm and moved me away from the Orbitron. "Let us show you to your new digs, president Commander."

I could see in her face, things I needed to learn. We walked along a path, next to a pristine lake of dark, blue water with everyone in our wake. In the distance I could see several of the escape pods, nestled together on the sands of a secluded beach. It all looked so idyllic—but I would soon find out about the severe challenges involved, in making Hera-soter our home.

∞∞

EPILOGUE

Dr. Beckett Conroy.
Executive Chairman,
Hera-soter Establishment Committee.
Project Establishment Log.
02-30-04. FE

—the enemy has surrounded the command pod. It is beginning to look as though they may overwhelm us.....

∞∞

Pick up on Beckett and Carla's story in the final book of the trilogy:

SURVIVAL OF A SPECIES.   Book Three: The Beautiful Planet

MORE BOOKS BY COLIN SETTERFIELD

The Helium-3 Conspiracy

Subduction Zone

Love Sweat tears

*The A-Mortal Gene

*The Beautiful Planet

The Memory Hunter. Special Agent O'Malley

Merlin's War   SpeciaL Agent O'Malley

The Omega File. Special Agent O'Malley

Operation Terra Firma. Special Agent O'Malley

Colin Setterfield